DUPED

HALLEE AND RUSS PATTERSON

Copyright © 2020 by Hallee and Russ Patterson

All rights reserved.

No part of this book may be reproduced in any form or by any electronic or mechanical means, including information storage and retrieval systems, without written permission from the author, except for the use of brief quotations in a book review.

Ebook ISBN: 978-1-73480-600-7

Paperback ISBN: 978-1-7348060-1-4

Large Print ISBN: 978-1-7348060-2-1

Memories have huge staying power, but like dreams, they thrive in the dark, surviving for decades in the deep waters of our minds like shipwrecks in the sea bed.

—J.G. BALLARD

PROLOGUE

Sometimes you must put yourself in the way of destiny.

— POLISH PROVERB

On the morning of February 7, 2004, when I made my usual eight-thirty call to my mother, she was having trouble speaking clearly—her words were coming out so fast.

"Gail, Zach just called me. He told me Lennox is in Chicago. She is staying at the Metropolitan Correctional Center." My mother told me this bit of news about my brother's ex-wife, Lennox, as though the accommodations were the Waldorf Astoria and not a prison.

"What is she doing there?" I asked, knowing this would be an interesting story.

"Zach told me Interpol found her in Costa Rica. Leave it to Lennox. What an exotic place to live, don't you think? Zach said she is going to be sentenced tomorrow. Dad and I are going. I hope I get to talk to her. I want to make a statement and vouch for her character. You don't need to help us tomorrow—Dad and I will be OK."

There was no way I wasn't going to be there. I had to see for myself, given my parents' talent for embellishing the truth.

Our story begins in the later part of the 1970s, when my brother Zach decided to do his medical school rotation in radiology in Florida. His plan was to enjoy the warm weather and be pampered by our parents. His life changed forever when he saw Lennox in the elevator. When he heard her British accent, he was enchanted. First, she asked him to play tennis, then in no time they were a couple. Not long afterward, our parents were called back to Chicago. They left Zach alone in the Florida condo—with the usual supply of unlimited funds.

Lennox, a stunning beauty from Toronto, was living in the penthouse of the same stylish Florida condo building as our parents when she came across them. My parents were ostentatious in their new-money ways and forever talking up the prospects of their unmarried son, the doctor.

My parents were strangely at ease with Lennox's latest development. Both of them enjoyed repeating the adventures they had with her and Zach to our relatives and their friends. This is how I learned about my brother's life. My role in our family was my parents' girl Friday. I was invisible to them until they needed something. I became a watcher, and in time, I learned a great deal.

"Zach told me we need to be at the Dirksen Federal Courthouse around one-thirty. Lennox's sentencing is set for two. Dad and I are planning on being there by noon, so meet us in the lobby," my mother informed me. I could feel her icy tone over the phone, she really didn't want me there.

"OK, will Zach be coming?" I asked.

"No, he said he was too busy to come on such short notice."

I was not surprised. Zach's current wife, Sloan, was jealous of Lennox and she would have forbidden him to attend. I marveled at the way my parents viewed Lennox. Because no one Zach ever dated was good enough for their prince, except for Lennox. She not only bewitched my brother, but my parents as well. They favored her even though she cost them millions.

I arrived at the courthouse at noon and waited for them. I was always amazed at how my parents entered a room. My beautiful mother, no matter the situation, dressed for show. There was no mistaking her among the harried lawyers in dark suits carrying stuffed briefcases or other people rushing through the lobby with their heads bowed low, all looking ordinary and common. On this day, my mother was wearing her full-length lynx fur coat and matching lynx hat set on a slight angle on her short dyed red hair, which accented her five-carat diamond earrings. She was also wearing her gold bracelets that jingled when she moved her arms and her signature six-carat diamond ring. She never carried a purse in the cold weather. But she did carry a fur muff, where she kept her lipstick, mirror, and handkerchief.

My father wore gray slacks and one of his many navy-blue sports jackets emblazoned with the crest he had designed himself, as well as a military rank pin on his collar. He had served in World War II as an army private but this did not stop him from wearing military pins symbolizing generals, lieutenants, or majors. On this day he chose to wear a gold oak leaf—a major's insignia. He felt these pins upped his status with the different police departments he sold uniforms to. When asked about his military service and experiences, he deflected from the subject.

As my parents entered, I could tell they were discussing the people in the lobby. They enjoyed critiquing people for sport, and I knew their routine by heart. My mother would say, "David, look at how terribly these people are dressed. They all look like farmers, or street people, or drug dealers. Do you think anyone here is a gangster?"

I could see my father searching me out. He acknowledged me with a wave and a nod of his head. My mother greeting was always the same. "What are you wearing? We really must take you shopping later." She never just said "Hello." I was fifty years old and she treated me as though I was sixteen.

"You are late," I said. "Do you have your ID? Remember, I told you to bring it this morning."

"No, I just have my lipstick, mirror, and a one-hundred-dollar bill." my mother responded in a huff as her eyes continued to wander around the room. "I don't need identification as long as I have your father by my side."

"I don't think they will let you pass without it, Mom. There are rules we have to follow."

"Nonsense. Gail, you don't know everything."

And with that said, she set out to prove me wrong. There was a long line in the lobby waiting to go through the security checkpoint. When the guards handed us the plastic containers for our personal items I looked at my father. When I get nervous, my voice goes high.

"Dad, should we take a cab back to your condo to get Mom's ID?"

"No, I will be able to get us through. Besides, look at your mother. She is so beautiful, who could refuse her anything?"

Then the show began. I had seen this performance by my mother so many times and still could not figure out how it worked. She stepped up to address the guards.

"Good afternoon, officer. I am Mrs. Dale of the Dale Uniform Company. Do you buy your uniforms there?"

"Yes, we do," responded the guard.

"Well, this is Mr. Dale." She stepped aside, moving like a magician's assistant waving her arms to present her husband.

My dad stepped forward to shake hands. The officers spoke of how often they shopped at Dale Uniforms and praised the prices and service at the store.

With the promise of free shirts and the patting of backs, the guards let my mom and dad through, never bothering to check their identification. I, however, had to show my driver's license and walk shoeless through the metal detector.

We did not know exactly where to go. We had never been in a federal courthouse before and I could tell my parents relished the experience—once again, Lennox was exposing them to a world they had only previously seen on television. As we approached the elevators, my mother saw a clerk rushing by.

"Excuse me, could you help us? We are looking for the courtroom where our daughter-in-law, Lennox Dale, is going to be sentenced." My mother's tone made it sound like Lennox was receiving an Oscar, not prison time.

The young man checked his clipboard and told us, "That's in courtroom 23B. Take the number two elevator to the 23$^{rd.}$ floor and turn left when you get off."

"This is the day we have waited for," my father said. We took a collective breath as he opened the heavy wooden door to the courtroom..

I was amazed at the size of the room and so were my parents.

"I can feel the importance of this room," said Mom. "Can't you, David?

We settled ourselves up front and I pulled out the news article about Lennox's arrest that my husband, Russ, had found on the internet. I must admit, I too was getting into the excitement of seeing Lennox again.

"Mom, Dad, look at what Russ found last night. The article says she is being charged with engineering a two-and-a-half million dollar fraud."

"Oh, Lennox looks so sad and pale in this photo," said Mother. "But really, even in a mug shot the girl is still stunning." Then, not missing a beat, she turned toward her husband and asked, "Do you think there will be a lot of people coming to see her? This courtroom is so large. I think it could hold more than a hundred people."

"Mom, Dad, don't you want to read what the news article says about her? It outlines what she has been up to these last ten years and the scheme to defraud her former employer."

"No, I know none of it is true." Mother turned her back on me. "David, I brought an ironed one-hundred-dollar bill to give to Lennox. Do you think I will be able to give it to her?"

"I don't know honey, Yes, I saw you ironing the money this morning." my father responded with a little smile on his face. He found his wife fascinating.

She prattled on, "You know, Zach told me Lennox really suffered in Costa Rica. When they arrested her, they took her to a prison there called Good Shepherd. How do you say that in Spanish, Gail?"

"El Buen Pastor. It's in the article I just showed you. It reads like a nightmare. Between the prison food and having to share a cell with at least five other women, I am sure it was torture for her." I said, as I rolled my eyes.

"Honestly, Gail, you have no compassion. Anyway, I hope I can talk to her."

"Wait, Mom, have you forgotten everything Lennox did, up to and including trying to have Zach killed? You know she's charged with some serious crimes here."

"First of all," Mother continued, "we don't really know what happened. She told us it was just a misunderstanding after she left your daughter's bat mitzvah. So be nice! Why did you come, anyway?"

"I want to see Lennox for myself. Besides, Zach asked me to come. And, he wants to make sure you and Dad will be OK."

"Well, if that is why you are here, please be quiet." She smoothed out the folds in her dress. "Do you think she will recognize us? Do you think she will be dressed in Chanel?"

At that moment, an official-looking woman entered the room from a door behind the judge's desk and headed for the small metal table on the other side of a partition. We watched as she shuffled her papers and pushed her oversized glasses up on her nose.

"David, I am going to go over to talk to her. I think making a statement on Lennox's behalf would be beneficial."

And with a nod between the two of them, Mother got up, opened the low gate that separated the visitors from the area of official business and crossed over to the other side of the room, and seated herself across from the clerk.

I noticed the involuntary movement of the clerk as she pulled her papers closer to herself and shrank away from my mother. However, Mother was adamant in her behavior, wanting the woman to listen to her, but the clerk ignored her. Finally, she gave up and came back to sit with us.

"That woman was so rude. Can you believe she would not talk to me?"

My father smiled down at his wife and said, "You tried."

Just then, a court official entered and made an announcement.

"The case of *The United States of America versus Lennox Dale* scheduled for two o'clock has been delayed and will not begin until four o'clock."

"David, that's two hours from now and we have already waited two hours."

Dad took his wife's hand and said, "Honey, we have waited ten years to see her. What is two hours more?"

Chapter One
OUR BEGINNING

> We must be willing to get rid of the life we've planned, so as to have the life that is waiting for us.
>
> — JOSEPH CAMPBELL

As in every family, everyone has a role. Mine was to serve. My mother decided my fate the moment I was placed in her arms. In her eyes, I would never be smart, would lack her beauty, never find love, and have no friends. Mother was a woman of great vision, as she often told me. She had a plan for everything and everyone. Zach, my older brother by four years, was to become a famous doctor, be fabulously rich, and marry a Jewish girl. Her plan for me was to be there to take care of her and my father.

My mother, Ruth Dale, had a morning routine of receiving calls from her children and her sister, Sara Lee. Sara Lee called first at eight. I was the next at eight-thirty, and finally my brother, Zach. Zach's call was to inform our parents of his daily plans. My call was to see if they needed me for the day.

My parents were nouveau riche, first-generation Americans, and high school graduates. Their parents were uneducated immigrants from Russia and Poland. Both sets of grandparents lived in a cloistered Jewish area in the south side of Chicago, where they had a hard time adapting to the new rules in the New World. I learned through Mother that Dad was the savior of his family.

"Your father is an entrepreneur, Gail. He cannot read well, but he is quick with numbers." The American dream was taking hold in the 50s, and a new reality was emerging for young families starting out. Many returning veterans were taking advantage of the GI Bill. My father was not one of them. He went to work for his father when he was discharged from the service and soon he was running his business. We moved out of Chicago's inner city when I was five and my brother was nine to a new development just north of the city.

Everyone's home was new, and all the neighbors on our block had a similar background story. The families were Jewish, from Russia, or Poland. The men were veterans who had fought in the Second World War. All the men worked in retail and all the mothers stayed home to raise their children. On warm summer nights, the families of the 6800 block of Keystone congregated on the street—the men leaning up against their Chevy or Ford station wagons engaged in conversation about their businesses or war stories, and the women huddled together pulling up weeds from their newly planted lawns. All the neighborhood children played bat ball or similar games on the tree lined street.

I felt my parents stood out. Dad resembled the other men because they were all Ashkenazi Jews, but what made him different was the way he spoke—he was animated. His face would light up and he seemed to do a little dance with his hands when talking about his new ideas for his businesses. He was driven to earn a lot of money, because he did not want to relive the poverty of his parents. Mother was more attractive than the other mothers, who looked drab to me. She was tall and stood straight with a perfect hourglass figure and shapely legs. Her exquisite sea green eyes contrasted perfectly with her thick dyed red hair which she wore in the "bubble" the hairstyle of the time.

Like my father, she seemed different from the other parents—more alive. Possessing an aura of excitement the other mothers didn't have. She was a master of conversation and charmed people easily never being afraid to approach anyone to start a conversation. Always feeling she was destined for greatness.

"You know Gail, I could have been an actress, but I married your father instead." She'd say this with a sigh and a slight bend at her shoulder. Dad was madly in love with her. I watched the way he looked at her, never quite believing his good luck. He loved her from the moment they met, and their love story shaped Zach's life, whether he wanted it to or not.

Chapter Two
THEIR LOVE STORY

> There is no greater agony than bearing an untold story inside you.
>
> — MAYA ANGELOU

President Eisenhower put his weight behind building the Interstate Highway System. Returning servicemen were purchasing cars and new suburbs were popping up along these expressways. Our suburb of Lincolnwood was a prairie before the exodus from Chicago began.

In our subdivision, all the homes had the same floor plans, but with different facades. They were split level with three bedrooms, one-and-a-half bathrooms. Leaving behind her beloved Humboldt Park and its familiar collage of European ethnic groups, Mother felt she was well on her way to realizing her dreams.

Mother was a planner; she had her house organized before we even moved in. "I just hired Nolan Didier, a top decorator in Chicago," she told her friends. "He has been taking me to the Merchandise Mart to look at furniture." Among other things, Didier recommended a white sectional sofa, to be encased in plastic, and a plush light gray wall-to-wall carpet for the living and the dining room. The carpeting and the plastic sofa made it clear that no one was ever to step into these rooms

—they were there just to be admired. Thirty years later, when Mother sold the house, I tried to remember if I had ever sat on any of the furniture or even gone into the living room.

The kitchen was our hub. It was a large room with a connecting dining area and a sunroom off to the side. In the corner of the sun room was my parents' prized possession—their twenty-four-inch Emerson color television set. It swiveled so they could also watch it from the kitchen table.

Our house had no need for bookcases, nor was the newspaper ever delivered, because my parents got everything they needed from the television, which was on 24/7. They never read to me growing up, instead, Mother enjoyed telling me stories about her mother and her life as a young girl. Retelling her family stories was her way to make sure her family members would never die, and indeed, through her, I could picture them vividly.

She wove her life tales together like historic myths. While recounting her stories, the tenor of her voice transformed to a melodic softness. She enhanced her stories with Yiddish words and songs, giving me a sense of the America she saw and experienced in the late 1920s through the 1950s.

Mother's favorite story to tell me, whenever I was driving them long distances was how she met my father. This story set the tone for our family, because the central fact was, it was her mother who made her *shidduch* (a Jewish arranged marriage).

"Gail, you must remember this story, if you forget even one name, we all die." She looked at me with the eyes of a wise woman talking to her apprentice that she really did not trust, but had no one else to tell. And then, her eyes left me to stare out into space as she launched into her family history.

"My mother's name was Tybee Marder. She lived in a small village in Poland called Grodner. At twenty-one years old, Tybee kissed her parents goodbye for the last time and boarded a ship sailing for Ellis Island. She was coming to America to marry her love, at the time when conditions in Poland were becoming dangerous for Jews."

Whenever Mother began her mother's love story, her manner was to hesitate, paying her respects to the memory of the departed, holding her thoughts for a moment. After this slight pause she continued, looking up with hopeful eyes. "I always marveled at my mother's courage in leaving her family. She spoke only Yiddish and Polish. She was coming to America to marry, Simon. They had saved their money to send Simon to America. He had been living in New York for three years before my mother was able to join him."

Mother took a breath, and her eyes seemed to cloud as she pictured her mother. Then, with a shake of her head and a scratch to the back of her neck, she continued. "When she arrived at Ellis Island and was processed, her future husband was late. Once he finally got there, she saw that he was dressed in the fashion of the day: straw hat, white spats, a high-collared white shirt, and a worn-out black suit. His attitude toward her had changed too. He was not happy to see her, not wanting a greenhorn from the old country. He rejected her at Ellis Island." Mother's habit here was to look down at her hands; her entire body seemed to crumble as she paused to reflect on the heartache she knew her mother experienced.

"Despite this, Simon was not totally dishonorable. He took her to stay with some friends. My mother was so disappointed that she wanted to die. Her thought was to jump off the Brooklyn Bridge. But, as fate would have it, she also had a toothache." This was another stopping point where Mother lowered her eyes, shook her head, then glanced over at me to make sure I was still paying attention.

I tried to imagine my short grandmother with her big breasts and heavy black shoes as a young girl walking the crowded, dirty streets of New York searching for a dentist's sign showing a tooth.

"The dentist she found was from Poland and spoke Yiddish. She told him her problem and like an angel he told her about a family in Columbus, Ohio. He told her he would write to them and she could live there and work for them at their tailor shop. Two weeks later, she got her answer and boarded a train to Columbus to live with Tanta Liskee Cohen, whose hair was so long it reached to her heels, and her *meshuge* (crazy) husband Mort. Well, my mother loved this couple, but wanted to get married. Tanta Liskee told her about a man living in Texas. She understood he was from her village back in Poland. George, my father, came to America because his mother had died and his father had remarried a wicked woman. He was a boy of sixteen when he hired on to work the steamer ship that docked in Galveston, Texas. From there, he went to work for the Rock Island Railroad. My mother wrote and George wrote back. The second time my mother wrote, she told George she did not intend to be a pen pal. Therefore, if he wanted to marry her, he should come to Columbus. And that is what he did. My mother was not in love with him at first, but by the time I was born, they were comfortable with each other."

And then Mother plunged into her story, how Tybee made her *shidduch* (a Jewish arranged marriage) and found her *bashert* (soul mate), David. This was her best memory, and she told it so animatedly that it never became boring. Mother was a wonderful impersonator, hunching to evoke Tybee who stood under five feet tall, and standing straighter and bringing her voice down several octaves to imitate David, occasionally stopping to look down at her hands in the way he so often did.

"For my birthday, your grandmother took me shopping for fabric for a new dress. She had stashed away house money to make me this gift." At this point she looked up to the heavens, remembering her wonderful life and mother, and then stared down at me as if to say, "What went wrong with us?" Continuing with a faraway expression on her face, she transported herself back in time. My dad patted her hand and smiled knowingly.

"Do you remember your grandmother Gail? She was perhaps five feet tall; I was six inches taller than her. We must have made a strange pair as we walked down the streets always holding hands. On this excursion, like every day of the week, my mother wore her standard gray, homemade, floral-patterned, belted dress she had made on her Singer sewing machine—this machine was her one extravagance. Her short, curly hair had always been gray, and her light gray sad eyes shone as if to *kvell* (to feel happy or proud) whenever she looked at me, her *shayna maidel* (pretty girl). I was dressed in a white cotton blouse and a well-worn skirt. My legs were bare except for white bobby socks and black saddle shoes.

"At the time, we had to take two trolley cars to get to downtown Chicago. The fact that we are now riding in a Rolls Royce should make you realize, Gail, how far we have come from that day." As Mother said this, she gave a wink to her husband, who was also listening attentively.

"To shop at Marshall Fields in those days was the height of elegance. The department store had everything you could wish for. Taking the escalator down to the fabric department, we could smell and see the colors and abundance of fabrics. We could hardly wait to start our hunt. David, do you remember this?" And with a scratch to the back of her head she continued.

"As we were nearing the sale section in the back, a young man came up to us. He asked us if he could help. When my mother looked at him, she forgot all about the fabric for my dress. Instead, she decided this was a chance to shop for a boy for me, someone with a steady job. I was a senior in high school and the next phase of my life was soon to begin. So, she turned to him, looked him up and down, and trying to be coquettish said, 'Oy, yes, can you help us?' and without skipping a beat asked, 'Do you have a girlfriend?'

"I was so embarrassed. My mother was always on the lookout for a match for me. She was always *kibitzing* (chatting) with people she met on the street or in restaurants, asking if they knew anyone who might be husband material. But she had never been so bold as to do her matchmaking in front of me.

"The young man looked down at my mother then shot me a look of approval. 'No, ma'am,' he replied with hope in his eyes. 'Wonderful!' said my mother. 'Perhaps you would like to come over to our apartment on Saturday night? You could bring four or five of your boyfriends too? Ruth, come over here and meet ... What is your name?'

'My name is Morris, but everyone calls me Morrie. Swell, I will ask a few of my friends'.'

"And with the arrangements made for the date and the time, my mother gave him the directions to our apartment. As we were leaving, we realized we forgot to buy the fabric. But it didn't matter: we had a party to plan. On the trolley ride home, we put our heads together and giggled as we relieved our conversation with Morrie.

'*Kina-hora* (to ward off the evil eye), Ruthy, just invite your not-so-attractive and not-so-smart girlfriends. You are beautiful, and I want you to be the center of attention. I want that you should shine.' That was her advice to me.

"I invited four of my girlfriends. My mother and father readied our apartment for the party by rolling up our threadbare rugs and borrowing a radio from our neighbors. Well, at eight o'clock Morrie came over with his friends and one of them was David.

"When the boys entered the apartment, I must be honest, I did not notice my future husband. I was so excited!" Mother looked over at my dad and shook her head as if to apologize. My dad smiled in return, reliving this experience with her. "We turned on the radio. Boys on one side, girls on the other—being in the apartment with my mother and father watching over us made mingling awkward. My mother went about assessing each young man as she tried to serve them her traditional mandel bread cookies and fruit punch. Suddenly, one of the boys suggested we go bowling.

"It was at the bowling alley that David made his move. He bought me a Baby Ruth candy bar. When I looked at him to say thank you, I fell in love." At this point, Mother always looks at Dad and their eyes connect and seem to twinkle with the knowledge that their match was made in heaven.

"We had a short courtship, mainly walking and talking in the park or in my parents' front room. We only dated five months before he was drafted into the US Army. Right before he was to be deployed overseas, he asked me to visit him. He was sent to Granada, Mississippi to do his basic training. I went with my mother and Kate, David's mother.

"I was so excited to take this trip with my mother and David's. The three of us boarded the Illinois Central Railroad at Union Station to go south. There were so many young boys in uniform waiting with their families and girlfriends to say goodbye. I can remember how exciting and terrifying the experience was. But I was so young, and my mother was by my side. I don't think I really understood the implications of this trip, but I believe my mother did. You know she was psychic, and so am I." I believe it is at this point that I would roll my eyes and feel intimidated. But she continued the story, never noticing me.

"Your father came straight to our hotel. I was looking out the window for him and when I saw him, I ran out of our room and into his arms. He spun me around just like you see in the movies and kissed me on the lips right in front of his mother and mine. When my mother saw him plant this kiss, the wheels of her brain started churning. She turned to your dad and said, 'David, I think you love my Ruthy. I think you should get married, right now.'

"My darling mother looked up at David with the purist determination in her eyes. Perhaps that's what prompted him to ask, 'Ruth, do you want to marry me?'

"And I said OK, because I could not think of anything better to do that day. Remember, I was young." At this point my mother's eyes would shine with laugher and she would scratch the back of her head remembering how adorable she was at eighteen.

"We were married on March 20th and the year was 1942. David's army buddy, Victor, stood as his best man and my mother stood at my side as my matron of honor. Your dad purchased a pink gardenia for me at the canteen and bought a twenty-five-cent ring at Woolworths. A rabbi married us in a church! The entire affair took less than ten minutes—there were many couples getting married because there was a war on and the boys were leaving. The next day, David left for Europe and I went back home to wait for his return."

With her story completed, my mother took a deep breath, took her husband's hands, and with a shake of her head said, "Don't you think I am the best storyteller? I really should have been an actress. I am so talented." My father looked down at her and smiled with pride at his beautiful wife and felt grateful for their good luck. Their love was eternal and who wouldn't want that?

It is this story that shaped my brother's life because who knew more about love and picking a life's partner than they did?

Chapter Three
AMBITION AND HARD WORK

I'm a great believer in luck, and I find the harder I work, the more I have of it.

— THOMAS JEFFERSON

My paternal grandfather, Esrael, boarded a ship from Kiev with his parents and older brother. On this voyage to Ellis Island, the two brothers found their wives. Esrael's bride, my grandmother, was named Kate. Esrael and Kate had three children.

My mother, as the self-imposed keeper of family legends, told me stories about my father's early childhood. "You know Gail, your father was not planned. Your grandmother was happy just having Bernice and Irv. It is a good thing they had your father because without him the family would have starved."

My father was a product of his time and culture, a street kid, a hustler, good with numbers, and always looking for a way to make a buck. After serving in the US Army in World War II, Dad arrived home with only the clothes on his back and his army discharge check. He had earned his high school diploma, however, learning had not been easy for him—perhaps today he would be labeled dyslexic. He made up for this shortcoming with an amazing capacity for doing financial analysis and math calculations in his head. Married, with no job and no desire to further his education after his discharge, his only prospect was to work with his father.

Esrael, whose first language was Yiddish, never wanted to assimilate. His used clothing store was typical of the neighborhood. It was located on an immigrant street where all the stores were in old dilapidated buildings. The store Esrael rented was on the corner of Roosevelt and Jefferson. It was a long, narrow, and dark space with no bathroom and a single light bulb hanging by its cord in the middle of the store. The used clothes were laid out in a cacophony on wooden boards laid over sawhorses. On these boards were his inventory of used men's pants, shirts, jackets, ties, socks, and shoes. Shoppers had to rummage through his goods. Esrael gave no customer service, just stood there watching for *gonifs* (crooks).

When Dad looked around at this *mishegas* (mess, craziness), he felt ashamed. He did not want to replay his parents' life of poverty and constant struggle. He had initiative and was driven to make a better life for his family. His first objective when he began to work with his father was to create order out of disarray by organizing the merchandise and styling the items to look more appealing and he showed a knack for window displays. But Esrael did not like change and constantly argued with his son. The two would end up battling every day over the proper direction for the business.

The famous Chicago shopping area in the 1940s was Maxwell Street. It stretched about a mile long from the Chicago River to the railroad yards and paralleled Roosevelt Road. It was a busy, thriving market from the turn of the century, where enterprising immigrants started their businesses selling anything from new to secondhand, legal, or illegal goods. They sold their merchandise from pushcarts, card tables, blankets, sidewalk kiosks, to the small stores that lined the street.

Sunday was the market's busiest day because stores run by Christians were closed. Dad could hardly wait to go to Maxwell Street Market early to see what the public was buying, meet with different vendors to learn which items were in demand, or which business had the largest crowd and why. The night before, he visualized the market and strategized each stop in his mind. He carefully orchestrated every move with the dealers he was going to approach.

Dad knew most of the store-keepers by their first name and had made a reputation for himself as a man who was to be trusted. For he observed his father's style of merchandising and realized the way to make a profit was to buy his merchandise cheap and then sell it for a reasonable profit, one had to be fair.

It was a game to him as he played on the Jewish merchants' emotions, knowing it was a Jewish trait never to be exact, 'Hi Ben, how is your business?' 'What's selling?' 'Have you sold out of anything?' 'Anything I should know?' His friendly line of questioning eventually garnered results. Dad's big break came from one of the vendors who told him about the hotels which were remodeling.

'Davy, I just learned the Palmer House is going to be remodeled. They have furniture and accessories they need to get rid of. Why don't you go over there and ask to speak to my nephew, Jeff? You might be able to work out a deal with him.' Oscar, the appliance merchant advised."

Dad learned that the large downtown Chicago hotels were paying waste haulers to remove their old furniture. These hotels were remodeling their lobbies and guest rooms after the end of World War II. He approached the hotel managers and offered to do them a favor by removing their old tired mattresses, tables, lamps, pictures, and chairs at no charge. The merchants on Maxwell Street were looking for cheap goods and paid cash on the spot. He exited the furniture resale business once competitors got wind of his ways, but the lessons he learned were to support him for the rest of his life.

Dad was looking for new sources to supply his father's used clothing business. Being in the US Army, he was familiar with the items given to him upon discharge. He learned that discharged servicemen were abandoning their duffle bags at the various Chicago train stations, bus, and airport terminals. Dad offered to remove these unclaimed items at no cost. Once again, he knew who would want the shoes, socks, shirts, and pants on Maxwell Street. Further, he noticed that some of the abandoned military coats resembled the jackets worn by the Chicago Police Department.

The US Army had trained Dad as a tailor. He had experience altering dress uniforms at the army's European headquarters. Buying a used sewing machine and taking a corner in his father's store, he figured out where he could buy the various patches and buttons needed to make regulation uniforms. Business took off, there were never enough uniforms to supply the growing Chicago Police Department or Chicago Transit Authority. He parlayed this scrappy start into Chicago's largest and most complete uniform store, the Dale Uniform Company.

Success begat further success. A few years later, a tip at a poker game led to his first investment, a shopping center. Soon, he had a small portfolio of high-rise apartments and strip centers worth millions of dollars. Finally feeling secure as a bona fide real estate mogul, Dad started taking weekends off from the uniform store.

My parents started renting summer cottages in Michigan, and eventually Mother convinced Dad to look at a Jewish resort community where she had friends. He purchased a summer home on a small lake in Wisconsin. He called it his Brigadoon.

Once Zach and I were on our way to college, they moved back to a very different Chicago, to a newly developed area of high-rises adjacent to the Magnificent Mile where all the big department stores were building their flagship locations. Mother was now closer to premium shopping and finding designer clothes which she bought on sale. Dad continued to indulge himself with a new car every year, topping off with a Rolls Royce for him and a Mercedes coupe for the love of his life.

It was time to live and enjoy! Taking a vacation in Florida one Thanksgiving, they were inspired to purchase a place to escape the brutally cold Chicago winters. They found it in the Hallandale area, north of Miami Beach, a predominantly Jewish community complete with kosher bakeries and delis. The Dales finally had it all.

Chapter Four
TRUE KNOWLEDGE EXISTS IN KNOWING THAT YOU KNOW NOTHING

What is a cynic? A man who knows the price of everything and the value of nothing.

— OSCAR WILDE

Zach was the only male heir to this fortune, and our family's world revolved around him: his athletic wins, his latest article in the school newspaper, and the classes he was taking. Now in his teens, his confident walk and his six-foot-one athletic frame gave him an air of success. His manner of dress also marked him as eccentric and unique. Wanting to project the appearance of a well-informed scholar, he came to family gatherings dressed impeccably. He accessorized with a weighty book under his arm. After greeting all the relatives with a kiss or a strong handshake, he seated himself, opened his book to read instead of participating in conversation. Members of the extended family forgave him all his eccentricities because he was David and Ruth's son, a respectful, handsome boy. He was their dream come true, their hope for the future, their prince charming.

Zach found our family dull, uneducated, and lacking culture. We never went to museums, concerts, theater, nor did we discuss current events. He aspired to be an intellectual, like the parents of his friends, who were doctors, lawyers, and engineers. At dinner, the only time our family sat together, Dad's evening conversation centered on his daily adventures at the Dale Uniform Company. Zach wanted to discuss current events as he did at the homes of his friends—to talk about serious issues like the environment or politics.

"Why can't we talk about what is happening in the world today?" Zach asked one day when he was seventeen and brazen enough to confront our father.

"What are you talking about?" Dad braced his hands on the Formica kitchen table to steady himself. His eyes were wide in disbelief. "I was talking about my day at the store. What does pollution have to do with the deal I got from Max on 80/20s pants?" Dad continued talking and eating, the television was blaring the evening news and Zach looked down at his book pretending he did not know us. I ate the meal all the while watching Walter Cronkite, never paying attention to what my father or what Mr. Cronkite were reporting.

We were conditioned to just sit, eat, and leave. We were never asked about our daily activities, school, or what plans we had for the weekend. Dinners took ten minutes from start to finish. Zach found every aspect of our ritual dinners appalling. He dreamt he was adopted and that his cultured and educated family from Europe were searching for him.

When Zach was a freshman in high school, he became obsessed with a history teacher who came from England. He loved to go to class just to hear him pronounce words. American English now sounded common to him. At dinnertime, he practiced European cutlery skills, turning his fork upside down in the British manner. He began reading classic English novels. Soon, he was speaking with an English accent, and then he started dressing in the old English fashion, wearing plaid jackets with ascots to school. Fortunately for Zach, he was able to run away to college, bankrolled by the very parents he was desperate to flee. He had a wonderful four years at this university, finding friends with whom he could share intellectual pursuits. He was free from his parents' voices.

Graduating with a bachelor's degree, then on the brink of a

master's, he still wasn't on track to earn that prized MD that mother predestined for him. But Vietnam changed all that. In 1969 the Selective Service System of the US had a lottery to determine how they would draft men born from 1944 through 1950. They placed birth dates in a wheel and spun it as you would to play Bingo. Zach's birth number was low, fifty-six. Since he was going to graduate that year, our parents got to work researching how they could spare their precious son from war.

First, Dad was able to use his influence with the politicians he knew in Chicago to get Zach into the US Air Force Reserves. And finally, Mother was able to convince Zach to go to medical school knowing it would keep him out of the draft and bring him home from the reserves. She learned from her Jewish network of friends about a medical school in Chicago known for accepting Jewish students whose parents were able to make large donations. Dad donated fifty thousand dollars on Zach's behalf and promised more in the future. Knowing medical school would keep him out of the draft for another four years, perhaps long enough to outlast the war, Zach was saved!

Thus rewarded, our parents redoubled their efforts for Zach. Once he started medical school, they purchased a studio condominium for him in the Old Town section of Chicago as well as a European sports car. They were determined to make his life stress free: no financial worries and a perfect life as they happily paid all his expenses.

Zach, never one to deny himself anything, was always dining out and buying whatever he wanted without so much as a second thought: suits with matching ties and handkerchiefs perfectly folded to fit in his suit lapel; guitars, then many other different types of string instruments; books, fiction, and nonfiction; tennis and golf equipment. He enjoyed both movies and theater. He never ever looked at the price. Therefore, Zach's bank account always needed to be augmented and Dad continually complained to Mother about Zach's spending habits.

"Ruthy, your son does not know the value of money," he would say at dinner, as I sat there and wondered why they never gave me money so freely.

"David, calm yourself. He is going to be a doctor. When he graduates, he will take care of us. Think of it as a good investment."

Chapter Five

PUT IN A GOOD WORD FOR A BAD GIRL, FOR A GOOD GIRL YOU MAY SAY WHAT YOU LIKE

— POLISH PROVERB

Then there was the question of a suitable wife.

My parents loved to shop, and their favorite thing to shop for was a potential mate for their son. My grandmother, Tybee, had made a successful match for them, so they felt they knew a thing or two.

"You know Zach, two heads are better than one," Mother told her son, adding with a bright smile, "and yours does not count." Zach would look down with a slight smirk whenever he got this stock treatment. He would shake his head and look up at her with what our mother thought were eyes of love.

It was their habit while out with friends, shopping, or eating out to scan any room for good candidates. If an attractive girl caught their eye, they approached her. Dad was even known to run across busy streets if he saw a potential candidate for Zach.

Saturday morning "Zach shopping" was the same every week. Mother went to the beauty salon on Friday for the works, then on Saturday morning, she spent extra time applying her makeup and choosing her best jewelry.

Dad's wardrobe never changed. He wore a navy-blue sports jacket with a white golf shirt and gray or tan slacks depending on the season. He loved jewelry too. He sported a heavy chained gold necklace and a gold diamond-studded bracelet to complement his diamond pinky ring. My parents were two peacocks spending the morning primping and dressing to make an impression. Once dressed, they left their 68th floor condominium and took the elevator to the lobby.

After a ritual breakfast at the nearby Ritz Café, they headed to Michigan Avenue. Mother linked her arm around her husband's as they walked with determination to find their targeted prey. On the street, random people stopped to compliment them, telling them what a handsome couple they made. They were used to hearing these compliments so they smiled down at these gawkers and give them a royal nod.

Entering their agreed upon store, they stopped at various locations to scan the area. "There, David, see the cute blonde standing by the cashier? I think she is in her twenties. She has good skin, and a cute body. I like the pin she is wearing. Do you think we should approach her?"

"Yes, she is lovely." Then he gazed at his beautiful wife, with her shining eyes. He could feel the excitement of the day.

Whenever they spotted a girl they thought appropriate, they observed her for a little while. Their initial criteria was beauty, and then how she interacted with her customers. A smile and a happy disposition were pluses. They judged her hairstyle, makeup, clothes, and finally, her voice. They listened to her as she conversed with her clients. Any nervous habits, like playing with her hair or a pen, eliminated her as a candidate. If the girl passed the test, they approached her and asked her a few questions. It was much like the Miss America interview, only they didn't have a microphone.

"Hello, my husband and I have been admiring you," Mother began.

"Thank you, can I help you with anything?" The girls they approached all took it for granted that they were beautiful and worthy of attention.

"Well, we were wondering, are you married?"

"No, why do you ask?"

"Well, we have an eligible bachelor son. He is studying to be a doctor and has no time for a social life. When we saw you, we thought you might be interested in meeting him." Mother did the interviewing. This approach actually worked, often enough.

My parents never thought to ask if they went to college, education was not important for them. They just had two deal-breakers: the girl had to be Jewish and she had to have good handwriting. Once the girl answered their questions and she passed their test, they got her phone number. The matchmakers returned home giggling. They always thought they had found the perfect girl.

"Zach, Dad and I found her today. Sheri works at the cosmetic counter at Neiman Marcus. She is so beautiful, great skin...." Then they described her features. This happened a couple of times per month and the stories changed very little. The girls they found were all very similar—in their twenties, thin, and many worked at department stores or restaurants. Sometimes they found prospective girls with their mothers having their hair done at local beauty salons.

My parents loved the hunt and their friends enjoyed hearing about it as well. None of them had the *chutzpah* (shameless audacity) to approach young women or men to fix up with their children. My parents were never disappointed when Zach called and said he didn't like the current choice, because that meant they could jump back into action.

"Hi Mom, I went out with Sheri," he told them in his tired voice. "No, I did not like her. She had the biggest big toe I have ever seen." The rejection always had some physical attribute. And after each report their quest continued with new vigor.

Chapter Six
THE CHATTERBOX AND THE SPY

Most people are other people. Their thoughts are someone else's opinions, their lives a mimicry, their passions a quotation.

— OSCAR WILDE

Chicago is one of the greatest cities in the world, but the winters are harsh. It is downright miserable with overcast gray skies and freezing rain, or snow combined with a strong cold biting wind off Lake Michigan. The sight of a clear blue sky is deceptive, because even then it's still freezing. Some say it is warmer by the lake, but that does not mean much. Even in the summer, the memory of bone chilling cold is never too far behind.

As the 1970s closed, sunnier climes called my parents. Real estate was affordable and people had money to spend. Florida was booming and developers were building high-rise condominiums along the ocean and intercoastal waterway. The ocean breezes were sweet. People were coming to Florida from the northern parts of the United States and Canada to retire and to escape the cold winters. Sunbathers knew little about the harm from the sun's rays.

With references from friends, my parents chose the Hallandale area north of Miami Beach. They bought in at a time when condominium development was hot. Buildings were going up fast, each building trying to outdo the next in amenities. Their building had an Olympic-size swimming pool with four tennis courts. The area had become a predominantly Jewish community, complete with kosher bakeries and delis. With this purchase, my parents felt they had it all: a luxury home in a high-rise in Chicago, a summer home in Wisconsin, a winter home in Florida, and their Rolls Royce.

"It's time to live and enjoy!" were Mother's comments to her girlfriends as she told them all about her new home in the Sunshine State.

The year was 1976. Zach was in his last year of medical school. The final year's curriculum consisted of six-week rotations in different types of medical specialties. His next rotation was in radiology and he felt he needed a change of scenery.

He had already contemplated doing his radiology externship at a hospital in Miami Beach before broaching the subject on one of his morning calls. Zach had a tired yet effective routine for these calls—I listened to him enact it whenever he wanted something. He acted the part of a sad, overworked child and played to our mother's emotions. Subtly and indirectly, he initiated that he needed something, then he was able to maneuver her into thinking that the solution to the problem was her idea. He knew she derived pleasure from knowing she was making his life better. Nothing was too good for her son; she could never deny him.

From her kitchen window in Hallandale, munching on candy from her goody drawer, Mother talked on the phone. She was never fully aware of the conversation and where it might be headed. The view alone made it hard for her to fully concentrate on the conversation with her son, who was on his way to becoming a doctor, her lifelong dream for him. She wanted him to have a secure profession providing him a good living and a fabulous lifestyle.

"So, tell me, how are you doing with your studies at the hospital? Have you met anyone special?"

Zach never bothered to answer these questions because he had learned they were our mother's way of talking to him. She never wanted him to meet anyone because she and Dad were having fun meeting beautiful girls and telling them about their eligible son. Not hearing a reply, she took a breath and went on.

"Your dad and I are having a great time furnishing the new place. I wish you could come down and see it. I know the area we are living in would be fun for you. You could use some sun. Don't you think you could use a break from your studies?" And when he didn't reply, she continued. "Oh, can't you manage a few days off? Dad will pay for your trip. I think a few days away from Chicago's winter could do you a world of good."

"I don't think I can get away from my studies for a few days. I'm working long hours at the hospital," Zach replied with his most dejected-sounding voice. He did not tell her that he had already applied and was accepted at a hospital near them. By the end of the conversation, he had Mother sending him a check for his ticket.

Before Zach's arrival, our parents' daily routine was to get up around seven, then set out to one of the many bagel/deli restaurants for breakfast.

"David, do you want to go to Three G's or Two Jay's this morning?"

For a dollar ninety-nine they enjoyed the breakfast special. Their next destination was to one of the flea markets. Just like the bagel restaurants, there were many to choose from: Monday was Del Rey Beach, Tuesday was Fort Lauderdale, and so forth. Having decided on a destination, they drove their Rolls Royce to the flea market and parked it among moderately priced American sedans. Feeling like newlyweds, they held hands as they went about looking for furniture and accessories for their apartment.

The rest of the schedule was high noon for lunch, and then an early bird dinner around five. When they returned to their apartment, they unpacked their treasures, assuring each other what terrific taste they had. Then, they joined their neighbors by the pool in the late afternoon to talk about their day. Chatty and social by nature, Mother talked about her new life in Florida and felt compelled to share her good fortune with anyone who listened. She never asked them about their day, instead, carrying on about all her amazing purchases at the flea market.

Dad's conversations were about his business, talking about his vast empire of uniform stores and his immense real estate holdings. He liked to embellish. A property he bought for a million always became five million in the retelling.

This behavior inspired gossip among the neighbors, "Those Chicago people have so much money. Did you notice her huge diamond ring and their Rolls Royce? But why do they only shop at the flea markets?"

Their story got around, and into this setting, Zach arrived. He was tall, dark, handsome, and smart; a man studying to be a doctor! A Jewish mother's dream for her daughter. A catch!

Mother changed their morning routine to include playing tennis. One day, as the three entered the elevator dressed for their tennis date, there was a young woman, thirty-something, going down with them. She was of medium height and wore a bright blue scarf covering her dark hair. She was dressed simply in shorts and a top. My parents later told me they could feel electricity coming from this woman's bright blue eyes, as they drilled into Zach, who was openly staring back at her.

The woman who they saw in the elevator that morning appeared at the tennis court during one of their volleys. Ignoring everyone else, she spoke only to Zach when their match ended.

"Hello, could I persuade you to hit some balls with me this afternoon?" she inquired, speaking with a strong British accent.

Zach had been a college tennis player, so the offer did not sound strange at first. Everyone wanted to play with him. What was strange was his quick response.

"How about three o'clock?" As soon as the words left his mouth he looked over to his parents for approval. They looked at each other with wide eyes and then gave Zach their parental nod. They spent the next few hours laughing about what he was going to find wrong with his three o'clock tennis date.

"Her name is Lennox. Do you remember seeing her the other day on the elevator?" Zach told his parents as Mother served him a light lunch of tuna fish. "She also has a condo in the building—actually she has the penthouse." he said this with a little sly smile, thinking this bit of news was impressive, " Lennox told me she is here with her three children and their nanny. She lives in Toronto, but she's from Scotland originally. Did you hear her accent? She told me she's here to take a break from her marriage."

Our parents took this in without a second thought. Zach was happy and that was all they cared about. He had so many dalliances, what was one more?

About a week later, Dad was called back to Chicago by one of his real estate business partners. My parents left Zach alone in the condo, with the Rolls Royce and ten thousand dollars in cash.

With our parents gone, Zach was free to live as he pleased. He had been lonely in Chicago, but now in Florida with Lennox, he felt renewed. Her British accent, and the way she carried herself were intriguing. Plus, she shared many of his interests. For the first time in his life he felt a real connection with a woman. She received the newspaper every day and understood current events. She enjoyed movies, concerts, and plays and she read books!

He took Lennox to well-reviewed restaurants and accompanied her to boutiques in the high-end areas of Miami Beach, Fort Lauderdale, and even Palm Beach. He felt they had an immediate bond; she was so comfortable and fun to be around. Lennox was so unlike the other women he had dated, and he felt she could become his intellectual equal. When he told her about his life in Chicago, she listened attentively. The fact that she was married was an added attraction—like forbidden fruit. Zach was enraptured.

By the end of March, Zach completed his rotation and had to return to the Windy City. I learned from Mother how much Zach missed Lennox. She told me they spoke on the phone several times a day, and in late April, Zach received *the* call. It was Lennox, saying she was lonely and had to be with him—she wanted them to start a life together.

Her plan was to leave the children in Toronto, in the care of two nannies. She was expecting a large divorce settlement, and the children. They would be secure, and could be together forever. Zach was so happy! He had finally found true love.

I'd been over at the condo when he called to give our parents his good news.

"Mom, is Dad home?"

"Yes, dear. Is everything OK?"

"Yes, for once everything is better than OK. Can you put Dad on the line too? I want to tell both of you my news."

"You sound so great." She commented with glee in her voice, "One moment, I'll get Dad."

Our parents were in their Chicago condo on the sixty-eighth floor. Their apartment had eight rooms facing Lake Michigan. However, they never took advantage of the lake views, heavy curtains covered their windows. They had hired a top Chicago designer and this was his style. Not knowing any better, they trusted him and therefore were never comfortable in any of the rooms except their bedroom and the kitchen, which they had decorated themselves with items from flea markets and TJ Maxx. Their kitchen had two yellow princess phones so they could look at each other and share conversations. It was fun for them to talk to their friends and family at the same time and give each other funny faces in response to what they had just heard.

"OK, we are both on the phone. We can hardly wait to hear your news." They nodded to each other in anticipation of the story Zach was about to tell them.

"I have fallen in love." Zach blurted out, unable to contain himself.

"Oh, honey!" Mother cooed. In truth, I knew she was upset. She wanted to find Zach his true love, just as Tybee had done for her. With a little cough and a weak voice, she asked, "Who is the lucky girl?"

"Do you remember the stunning dark-haired English woman who asked me to play tennis?"

"Yes, of course. You told us she was there to reevaluate her marriage. Didn't you also say she had children?"

"Please do not get upset, Mom. Lennox is her name. She's coming to Chicago next week. I want you to get to know her. We are very happy together. I am *really* happy. We want to get married."

She did not want to upset her son, but Mother couldn't help herself as she blurted out: "How will you get married if she's married now? What about the children?"

"Don't worry. Lennox has it all worked out. She told me her

husband wants a divorce too, so the divorce will be quick. The three boys will come to Chicago to live with us."

When they hung up the phone, they sat quietly with their heads bowed looking at their hands. I felt confused but happy for Zach. It was all happening so quickly.

"I remember this girl, she was very pretty," Mother reflected.

"I remember her too," said Dad. "I think she had an English accent. We first saw her on the elevator and then at the tennis courts. She is very beautiful." Being beautiful was very important to him.

"Yes, but I never remember seeing her with children. It is so strange."

Dad, always in agreement, just nodded his head and looked down. They decided to stay neutral. They wanted to find Zach his wife; they could fudge a little. Her being in their condo building did give them the feeling they had something to do with the match. They made up their minds that this was just as good.

Zach called a few days later to let them know he was bringing a special guest over to visit.

Chapter Seven

SHE COULD SPEAK AND SAY NOTHING OF IMPORTANCE, BUT SAY IT WITH WIT AND GRACE AND EXPERTISE

I can resist everything except temptation.

— OSCAR WILDE

Zach's twelve hundred square foot one-bedroom apartment had a view of the Chicago Gold Coast, Loop Skyline, and Lake Michigan as an eastern border. The main benefit was that it was located right next door to the hospital where he was doing his residency.

After arriving at Zach's small condo, Lennox wanted to see where his parents lived right away. She was curious about their prestigious address.

Mother told me Lennox's eyes kept darting around their apartment, which she had attributed to nervousness, or everyone's excitement. My parents referred to their condo as their "home in the sky."

After seeing this residence, she was eager to take a weekend trip up to our parents' summer home in Wisconsin, near where I lived in Lake Geneva. I would finally get to meet this enchanting woman everyone was *kvelling* (bursting with pride) about.

Zach called me to let me know his plans, "Gail, I have some time off tomorrow. Lennox wants to meet you and see Mom and Dad's home in Genoa. How would it be if we trotted over in the late afternoon?"

I thought to myself, "'trotted over,' what an expression!" It was so like him that I had to smile.

"OK, Zach. Remember, I am trying to sell our house, so I am having a garage sale. Could you come earlier and help?"

I knew he wouldn't, but I held out hope that perhaps Lennox had changed him. I dreamed we would become more like my cousins who were always there for each other.

"Well, you know I am working at the hospital in the morning. I think we will come around dinnertime, maybe around five-thirty. We can have dinner in Williams Bay."

"OK, do you want to spend the night at the house? I have an extra bedroom."

"No, I think we will drive home after dinner. It's not that far," Zach replied.

I knew he was not going to be driving home, and that he was not going to be working in the morning at the hospital either. I already understood his routine, but sometimes I liked to test him. I had learned never to say anything to confront him because I never won.

When Zach arrived, I was just closing the garage sale. He stepped out of his black Sterling sedan and waved. I watched as my brother went around to the passenger side and opened the door for Lennox. As I watched him extend his hand, out bounced a beautiful, smiling woman. The weather was gray and overcast, yet it seemed to enhance Lennox's porcelain skin, giving her a luminescent glow. Her dark brown hair was worn in long curls and was adorned with a white tam hat placed coquettishly on the side of her head. I noticed right away that her eyes were the same color as my brother's, an icy blue.

My girlfriend, Faith, was helping me that day. She was also interested in meeting Lennox after all the stories she had heard from me. She said, "She looks like Snow White," but then I heard myself say, "Maybe more like the evil witch who delivers the poisoned apple." Faith gave me a funny look. But I was only a little surprised to feel those words slip out. Something felt wrong right away. I just didn't know exactly what.

Faith and I were wearing layers of old clothes, after spending a gray, frosty day working a garage sale, we did not look our best. In addition, I was six months pregnant. Lennox was wearing tight jeans with a form-fitting light blue sweater which upset me right away because I felt fat. Both Faith and I suddenly felt very aware and uncomfortable in our appearance as Lennox came up the driveway. We looked like sloppy suburban housewives, while she was every inch the elegant socialite.

"Oh, Gail, I am so excited to meet you at last. Zach has told me so much about you. I am sure we are going to be wonderful sisters-in-law." As she kissed and hugged me, she spoke in a heavy English accent. I looked at my girlfriend and we both suppressed a laugh.

"Hello Lennox, I am happy to meet you too. We are just closing. I know it's cold. Go inside Russ is preparing hot chocolate for you."

My husband, Russ, gave them a tour of the home we were selling and then served the hot chocolate and some cookies he had just baked. When I entered, they were sitting in the living room chatting.

"I just took Lennox to see Mom and Dad's house. It looks a little spooky all closed up for the winter."

"Yes, it does. Mom likes to put white sheets on all the furniture and lamps. She stores them in the hall closets in the summer. It took us hours to complete the job."

"I thought the setting was lovely," Lennox added, "the way the house was built in a little valley with the lake behind it and the tennis court to the side. The house appeared inviting. I can't wait to see it in the summer." she said as she batted her eyes at my brother, I think I rolled mine.

My brother was affectionate with his girlfriends in front of me, but with Lennox, they were not only touching and kissing each other, they were playing private word games that made me feel even more excluded and uncomfortable. An hour went by, and Zach announced they could not stay for dinner. He told me he had to make rounds early the next morning.

Why did I dislike Lennox, considering I had just met her? It started with Zach's phone call to our parents informing them of his love interest. During this call Mother went into her inquisition mode.

She wanted to know as much as Zach was willing to tell her about his new love. One of her most important questions related to Lennox was her three children.

"Gail, I am so excited. Zach is in love." When she had hung up the phone with Zach. She needed a little time to process what she had heard. And she felt she needed to get me up to speed with his life, never one to filter her thoughts,

"You know, Zach met her in our building in Florida. They fell in love the moment they looked at each other in the elevator—isn't it romantic? Lennox is from Toronto, but she was born in Scotland. She owns the penthouse condo in the Hallandale building. She is married but is getting a divorce," Mother took a short breath and then said, " Can you believe she is coming to Chicago this weekend! Zach could be a married man by May. Zach told me her husband wants the divorce too and, oh yes, she will have custody of her children. Zach told us she has three sons, ages six, four, and two. I am going to be a grandmother!"

"Yes, I know you are going to be a grandmother," I replied. "I am pregnant."

"Yes, but I mean to three gorgeous boys!" Mother exclaimed, forgetting about me as usual.

"What!?" I kept asking myself what kind of a woman can walk out on three young boys, and wondering why my parents didn't. What was I missing?

Lennox's introduction to the Chicago Dale clan was at Passover. Aunt Bev and Uncle Irv hosted the event in their modest home in Lincolnwood. The family was already settled at the table waiting patiently for Zach to arrive and introduce Lennox. As would become Zach and Lennox's custom, they arrived about an hour late, though nothing was ever said to Zach about his tardiness.

We were all seated at the table listening to Mother tell us about Lennox when the doorbell rang. I noticed my family sat up straighter, stopped talking, and with our eyes toward the door, we all waited to get a look at the woman who stole Zach's heart. Aunt Bev rushed to the door as though she was opening it for the prophet Elijah. There stood Zach and Lennox. The family then took a collective breath and rushed to the door to greet them.

Zach came dressed in his usual manner—a bow tie and a plaid sports jacket—and he was carrying a pipe, his new eccentricity. Lennox came dressed as a religious Jewish woman, in a dark blue checked skirt, the hemline at her ankle, a white blouse with a lace collar, short lace white gloves, and to top it off she had a doily head covering pinned to her hair.

"Does she expect us to think she is pious?" asked Judith, the most religious of the cousins.

"She is definitely different from the other girls Zach has brought to family gatherings," replied Judith's sister, Diane.

As Lennox entered the small room, she filled it with her presence. Zach introduced her to everyone. Aunt Bev thanked her for the white lilies she had sent. Giving a gift to the hostess was a gesture we were never taught. Suddenly, my cousins and I felt uncomfortable and a bit ashamed.

When the family began the service, Lennox stole the show. Uncle Irv conducted the service from the head of the table. As he handed out the Haggadah he had chosen for this years' service, he looked at our small family seated at the long table with our faces uplifted to his.

"I want to thank God for bringing us all together. I am very grateful for our family and for our new addition, Lennox. So, Lennox, would you like to begin reading first?"

"Yes, but first don't you want to light the candles and recite the blessing over the matzah?" Lennox corrected him.

Then she began reading from the Haggadah, able to pronounce all the difficult Hebrew words. She impressed all the aunts and uncles. They saw her as a rose among thorns. Here was a woman who dressed appropriately, could read Hebrew, and seemed to really enjoy the traditions of their Jewish heritage. Unlike their children, who only came out of obligation and who giggled, interrupted, and talked through the service. Each year, Uncle Irv tried to find Haggadah's that he felt would be interesting. As the years went by, he found Haggadah's that were shorter and shorter because everyone wanted to get to the meal and leave. But not anymore!

Zach had found a mate who met all the family's criteria. The cousins liked her fashion sense. The aunts and uncles liked the fact that she seemed to like them. Everyone forgot what they had heard about her past and instead saw her as the future. Zach had done it—what a find!

Chapter Eight
AN ENCHANTING LIFE

A liar can go around the world but can never come back.

— JAMES CONROYD MARTIN

Once a week, our parents met Zach and his soon-to-be-wife for dinner. They deferred to Lennox on the choice of restaurant. Mother loved being exposed to the new, hip places and to be privy to this part of her son and Lennox's life. However, Dad was uncomfortable at these restaurants because he never understood the menu.

Every one of their dinners started off with Lennox and Zach ordering cocktails or an expensive bottle of wine which our parents never drank because they preferred their sodas. Dad knew these evening meals with his son and Lennox would be expensive and he was the one picking up the check. He complained to me about the high costs, but went along, knowing that these evenings with his son made his wife extremely happy. And indeed, she bubbled over with details when we spoke the next morning.

On these calls Mother stressed how elegantly Lennox dressed and what an entertaining conversationalist she was. Telling them stories with funny anecdotes about people she met that day. I listened as Mother fawned over her.

Mother told me after Lennox had a few drinks, she loosened up and told them what she knew they wanted to hear—stories about her past. Mother, never one to hold back on any question, asked about her life in Scotland and Toronto. However, Lennox only shared little fragments of her past before turning the conversation back to the Dales.

"I grew up in the fourth largest town in the center of Scotland, called Wishaw, in the county of Lanark," Lennox's eyes sparkled as they zeroed in on Ruth when she related her past, knowing Ruth was hanging onto every word.

On my eight thirty call Mother caught me up on what Lennox told her the night before. Lennox's stories sounded to me as though they were torn from an encyclopedia, or a Chamber of Commerce brochure.

"My family home is set in a very beautiful place. When I was young we played outside because the lowland climate is temperate. The winters are mild with light rain and occasionally snow and the summers are delightful with warm southwestern winds."

"We lived in a small two-bedroom cottage on the edge of town. My mother, Rose, did not work. She was a housewife like you, Ruth, occupied with her three girls." Lennox never mentioned her father, and Mother was too intimidated to ask.

At first this was as clear as Lennox got about her family life. Her stories were sprinkled with a few facts, and seemed to have a beginning and an end, but the middle was fuzzy. "Oh, enough about me," she would say. "You look beautiful tonight Ruth. Is that a new outfit?"

Mother wanted to understand her son's love interest, but she could probe no further. She knew no one from Scotland, England, or Toronto to inquire about Lennox's past. My parents had no close friends in their Florida condo, therefore she had no one to gossip with. Mother hoped her intuition would help her figure out what Lennox's words did not supply. Months went by and then Mother would be given another nugget about Lennox's past.

"I grew up in Scotland, and moved to Canada when I had just turned eighteen," she told them at dinner one night. She wore trendy clothes; her hair and nails were always perfectly coiffed. Her new lapis lazuli contacts beamed at them. Her snow-white complexion was framed by her full dark brown hair which fell in waves to her shoulders. They gazed at her and did not care about her past. She was so lovely to look at. They were happy Zach found her and he was happy. However, a feeling of doubt and unease grew with time, because her stories never quite matched up.

On another evening Lennox continued her creation story, "Yes, you know I was born in England. My parents had a small cottage there. It was such a small provincial town. My mother told me I was a handful because at sixteen they shipped me off to relatives in Canada."

"Oh, I thought you were born in Scotland. And you came to Canada at eighteen," Mother remembered her saying, trying to clarify from past stories.

Lennox glared at her and pretended she did not hear her comments. To calm Ruth, she placed her hand on top of hers in a patronizing style and spoke in her most endearing voice, "Ruth dear, you do realize Scotland is a part of England. It is like saying I was born in Illinois or the United States—you know they both refer to the same place." Then looking down at her lap, Lennox composed herself. "Did I tell you Ruth, how beautiful you look tonight?" and that would be the end of her story for the time being.

Lennox picked up the narrative again the next time out.

"When I was a young girl, I felt something was not right in my family. When you meet my sisters, you will see that I don't look like them at all. Karson and Anna look like they come from the country. You know—sturdy, brunette women who would have made excellent farmers wives." Lennox gave out a little laugh at this recollection.

"They never liked to go to the city with me. We really had nothing in common. Remember, I told you I don't look anything like my sisters. Well, I don't act like them either. They are both rather shy, quite like wallpaper. I must admit I caused trouble for my parents. I loved to go out at night, but in our small town there really was nowhere to go. I realized there was no future for me in this village. At this time I was only thirteen years old and the only job I was qualified for was babysitting. I heard about a wealthy family in Motherwell. The family who hired me had two little girls, they traveled extensively with them. I became their *au pair* in the summer months. I traveled with them throughout Europe for three years. This family only stayed at five-star hotels."

Aha, thought Mother, who felt she was psychic. Surely this experience among the rich exposed Lennox to a world she had only read and perhaps dreamt about. She must have soaked up this world like a sponge and did everything in her power to have this type of life for herself.

"When I had to return to my family at the end of each summer, I became discontented," Lennox continued. "At sixteen, they sent me to live with my mothers' sister and husband in Toronto."

This part of the story Mother was familiar with, but she could not understand if Lennox finished high school, yet she was afraid to ask. Lennox had said that her uncle found her a job with a dentist. And when she became a dental hygienist, she met Steven, her first husband. When Mother asked her where she went to school to learn the trade, Lennox turned her head and her icy-blue eyes focused narrowly on Mother's. Mother realized immediately that she had made a mistake in questioning her. She would do anything to placate Lennox and not anger Zach.

Most of the time, Lennox seemed to enjoy telling her life story to the Dales. She relished the way they took everything she told them at face value. So, after a pause, she looked at Zach and his parents and decided to continue.

"Well, Steven was one of my patients. He came in to have his teeth cleaned regularly. In fact, he was one of many young men who came in and asked for me. I was the best hygienist in the office."

Mother nodded her head. She believed Lennox would be successful at anything.

"I had been living with my aunt and uncle for two years and I was ready to move out of their house. They were very kind, but I was now eighteen years old and I wanted a taste of the wider world. So, I guess you could say it was a youthful dream that propelled me to marry. Steven and I got along very well in the beginning."

Lennox's facial expression changed from serene to dispassionate.

"You must understand, Steven was nice and very kind at first, but you know how things can change."

"Oh yes," Mother reacted in the flippant way of a person eager to learn more of a story. Russ and I had been included in their dinner plans this evening because it was my birthday. I was sitting there watching and listening to this interchange as though I was on a cloud looking down at my family, because I know I was an invisible presence to them. I heard my mother say "And what did Steven do for a living? Did he have family in Toronto?"

"So many questions, Ruth. Well, Steven owned his own paper company; he had inherited it from his family. He was an only child and both his parents had passed away. We only dated for six months before we got married."

"Steven is Jewish. As you know I converted to Judaism and our children were brought up in the Jewish faith. I enjoyed the religion so much that I became active in the temple. When I left Steven, I was the president of the sisterhood." she told us with a proud smile. "We had status in the Jewish community of Toronto."

In this role, Lennox had plenty to do, and of course many people to meet. She told us how her relationship with her husband shifted. Explaining after ten years they had nothing in common. I sat at the table and watched Lennox maneuver Zach and our parents, I felt she was capable of changing like a chameleon. I was never sure of how I felt towards her. Mother was always boasting to her friends how smart and fun Lennox was to be with. However, when I listened to how she played with my family's emotions, I wondered why I never caught the Lennox drug. I understood how her attributes were mesmerizing my family. One: She had boundless energy that matched my mother's. Second: When she told a story, she matched my mother's ability to hold the listener's interest. Third: She was beautiful to look at. And, Fourth: She always had the perfect response to any question.

Lennox was thirty-three years old and in her prime when she entered our lives. As I listened to her stories I came to understand her three young boys hampered her active lifestyle even though she had two live-in nannies to take care of them. When the boys came to Chicago, they stayed with us. On the few times we spoke, she confided to me that she was tired of the cold weather in Toronto and she was searching for a way out of her marriage. Looking into the building boom going on in Florida, she ultimately wound up seated by the pool overhearing Mother prattling on about her life and her gorgeous unattached doctor son.

At one of their dinners she told my parents, "Steven and I were married for ten years when our marriage started to show strains. With the birth of our third child I realized I was not happy. I heard about the building boom in Florida and I asked Steven if we could buy a condo there. We purchased the penthouse as an investment. But the real reason I wanted to escape to Florida was to rethink our marriage. I felt time away from Steven would help me see things more clearly, and then I met Zach."

Zach took hold of Lennox's hand and they looked into each other's eyes for a long interlude.

"I am sure Steven will let me have the Florida condo in our settlement," she finished, with a sweet smile.

Mother wanted to say, "What about the children?" but was afraid of the response she would receive from Zach. Never wanting to anger her son and wanting to believe her future daughter-in-law, she just smiled with a touch of sadness in her eyes. There was something about Lennox that she could not understand, some unattainable feeling, like waking up from a dream that you want to remember but it fades before you can. You just know something isn't right, but you have no way to prove it. At some point in their evening meal, Lennox complimented Mother about her hair or clothes, or asked Dad about his business. Once the conversation turned to his business, his stories began, and Lennox's past was left for another time.

Chapter Nine
THE DIVORCE PROMISE

Crimes, like virtues, are their own rewards.

— GEORGE FARQUHAR

Mother wanted the fairy tale of love to continue for her precious son, but Lennox remained a mystery. Mother was never sure of anything Lennox told her because there was no way of confirming anything. When she asked Zach on their morning call for details or clarification, he never answered, leaving Mother to feel that she had overstepped her boundaries. Zach gave Lennox credibility. Mother trusted Zach so much that anything he told her, she decided had to be true.

Lennox told us that once the divorce was settled, which could take a year, she was going to receive a huge divorce settlement and custody of her three sons. This statement was music to Dad's ears. He was tired of financially supporting his thirty-five-year-old son. He had a little red book where he kept track of his financial gifts to both Zach and me. He checked the book periodically to remind himself of how generous he was—Zach's tally by then included multiple tuitions, donations to schools, condos, cars, and so on. Dad was happy to keep the couple afloat while they waited for her divorce to be completed. But the one-year wait was now stretching into three.

One day when Zach made his obligatory nine o'clock call, Mother was armed with questions.

"Zach, Dad told me you are going to Canada with Lennox tomorrow. He said you were going to accompany her to court. After three years, it's about time you went with her. I feel you need to see for yourself what is taking the court so long to give her the divorce. Do you think you might meet her husband?"

She waited for Zach to reply, but she did not hear anything from him on the other end of the phone, so she went on, "Do you think Dad and I could come along? We have never been to Toronto and perhaps she could show us around. I'd like to meet her sister and the aunt and uncle who took care of her. I would like to see the places that she talks about when we are together."

It was becoming important for Mother to see for herself Lennox's home city of Toronto and to meet her friends. She was curious to know more about this woman who meant so much to her son. My mother felt that she and Dad were invincible and could intervene in any situation to provide a solution.

"No, Mom, you will not be able to come with us. Lennox told me the proceedings were only open to her and her soon-to-be ex," he said, with an inflection of happiness in his voice. He was given assurance from Lennox that this was to be the last visit to Canada and she would be granted her settlement.

"She said she is not sure if I will be allowed into the hearing room. However, she wants me to go with her for support."

The next day, Zach called Mother from the hotel in Toronto. "Lennox told me it was horrible. When her divorce case was over, she called me and I went to get her at the courthouse. Can you believe Steven hit her after the court proceeding? She told me he has a terrible temper and he did not get his way, so he hit her! I have ice on her arm now. She also has a huge bruise above her eye, because she fell. No one helped her either. The court did not issue a final decree and Lennox has to return next month."

"What does Steven look like? Is he a big man?" Mother asked. My parents looked at each other, concerned, as they listened from their matching princess phones at the Chicago condo. "What did the judge do when he hit her? Poor thing. What are your plans now?"

When they heard the next part of Zach's story, they were even more confused.

"I wasn't there. I was waiting in our hotel room for her to call me. Lennox told me I could not accompany her. But now I wish I had gone to protect her. I could have at least waited in the lobby of the courthouse or outside of the courtroom. We will be returning to Chicago tomorrow afternoon. I will be in touch then."

When the couple returned home, Zach called and reported to them how Lennox had been wronged, telling them the story that Lennox told him of the proceedings.

"Steven screamed horrible things at her in court. As they were leaving, he caught up to her in the hall. That's when he hit her. I asked her why no one helped her. She told me she was walking out alone. Lennox is so brave and her husband is a bastard. Can you imagine him hitting her? I don't understand." Zach took a deep breath and continued, "Lennox told me her lawyer presented her case and now we have to wait for the judge to make his ruling."

It took six years for the judge to rule in Steven's favor, Lennox received nothing. Steven was not going to hand over their sons, nor was he going to give her a cash settlement. Zach had to appeal to our parents and again they opened their checkbook. Paying all of Lennox's court costs, including her personal expenses when she flew to Toronto. They rationalized it as an investment in Zach's happiness. At least they could close this chapter and finally get Zach married to the love of his life.

After Lennox's divorce was finalized, Mother and Dad were given the go-ahead to plan a wedding. Mother was thrilled to finally see her son married and she wanted to make the day special. She booked the small ballroom in the private club at the Ritz Carlton. They invited a few close friends and relatives. Mother had hoped to have Lennox's family attend, but it was not to be. Lennox told them her mother was ill, and her father would not leave her. In addition, neither of her sisters could come. One lived in England with two small children and the other was in Canada. Both claimed it was too short notice and could not make the necessary arrangements quickly. She had no one from her family at the wedding to represent her, not even a friend. Mother could not understand. Lennox had elegant manners, and was fun and exciting to be with, yet after living in Chicago for six years she had no friends.

One of Mother's friends had been intrigued with Lennox. Sylvia, was also from England and had found Lennox charming, so she invited her out for lunch to celebrate the upcoming wedding. Mother was hoping her friend could find out more about Lennox's childhood and how she ended up married in Canada.

Sylvia called the next day to say she did not think Lennox was the right girl for Ruth's only son. In her opinion, Lennox's stories seemed incomplete.

"There is something about her that doesn't feel right. She's too quick and her stories don't make total sense. I'm not sure what it is exactly, but something isn't kosher. Do you think they could wait? I'd like to contact some of my relatives in England to look into her background for you."

Mother replied in a huff, "What are you saying, Sylvia? The wedding is next week. Zach is so happy! I'd never do anything to jeopardize his happiness. He has waited a long time to find someone he could love. Do you know my girlfriend Sally once said to me she thought he was gay?"

The wedding took place on a Saturday afternoon. Mother had arranged for our family's rabbi to officiate. The bride had chosen an elegant cream suit complete with her signature gloves and hat. The groom was given a black tuxedo from Father's store and he accented it with a blue shirt and matching plaid cummerbund, pocket handkerchief, and bow tie.

It was a traditional Jewish service with Zach breaking the glass, signifying "as this glass shatters, so may your marriage never break." With a *mazel tov* (congratulations or wishing good luck), the couple went off for their honeymoon to Victoria Falls, Canada.

When they returned, Lennox started shopping and redefining herself. Now living in Chicago full time, she concentrated only on herself. To me, her transformation seemed predestined. When Zach was in college, he played the guitar, and his favorite tune was a song about a sailor who fell in love with a young beautiful woman:

> *Come all ye young sailors and take a lesson from me.*
> *And don't fall in love with the first one you see.*
> *Make sure they're complete from their heads to their toes,*
> *Don't be fooled by the machinery of nineteen years old.*
> *She took off her right leg an inch above her knee*
> *And on her left hand she had fingers but three*
> *And on her right shoulder a hump to behold*
> *Don't be fooled by the machinery of nineteen years old...*

The song goes on to talk about how this woman of nineteen takes off all her body parts and in the end, she is just a shell. Lennox started with cosmetic caps on all her teeth. Then, at a time when this really wasn't done, she worked out three times per week with a personal trainer who came to their apartment, and she whittled herself down from a size ten to a size four.

She decided to make her eyes bluer, becoming an early adopter of colored contacts. She always had a healthy glow, but when asked if she had been on a holiday, she never admitted to her use of her personal tanning bed.

To complete her metamorphosis, she had extensions, or hair fillers, as they were known in the 80s, attached to her hair, which gave her a lush mane that fell to her waist. And then, she changed her hair color from dark brown to auburn red, which was similar to Mother's and drew her admiration.

Mother and Dad were thrilled with Zach and Lennox—they made a stunning couple. Mother was known for her head-turning entrances, but she could not compete with her daughter-in-law, a true showstopper. When Lennox entered, it was as though the air was sucked out of the room. One of Lennox's new favorite expressions was, "You can never be too thin or too rich," said with a wicked smile and a toss of her fake red hair.

But Lennox was not quite done with herself. Her final touch

came right after our parents held a party for Zach's medical school graduation and their announcement of the medical practice they purchased for him. They wanted to share this moment with their family and friends to showcase how their son was on his way to great things.

They planned a lawn party at their summer home (a Jewish resort community) in Wisconsin. Their house faced a small lake where they owned a small fleet of boats. They had built a tennis court on the lot next to their house for Zach, hoping it would lure him to visit more often.

On the day of the party, the weather was beautiful, the sun was shining, and there was a warm breeze off the lake. All of my parents' friends and relatives from Chicago, Wisconsin, and Florida were invited, but there were no friends of the celebrating couple attending except for the surprise visit of Lennox's father, Peter. We were told he flew in from England the day before. Peter was short and stocky and had an uncanny resemblance to Winston Churchill, leading Russ and me to joke that he was hired from central casting.

Peter came to the party dressed in a three-piece gray suit buttoned over his protruding belly, his complexion was pale under a silver circle of tidy hair. He kept a cigar and a glass of Scotch in his hand the whole time. When Dad tried to talk to him about his life in England, Peter, just like Lennox, was evasive. Lennox once told us he was a plumber, then she told us he was a bookkeeper for a plumber. Lennox told my father that he had a penchant for the ponies and that is really how he made his money. But Peter was aloof and busy drinking, so no one really learned anything about him.

The morning of the party, Zach woke up brooding. Lennox was nowhere to be seen. This was a six-bedroom ranch house but not so large that people could disappear. Mother spent the morning fussing around Zach. Her excuse for him, as always, was that he had to eat a good breakfast and then he would be civil. But even after a good breakfast, he remained unhappy.

"Our gift to you is a trip to wherever you want to go," Mother announced with Dad standing by her side at the climax of their party. Our parents' faces were flushed, they were so proud to be able to announce this to their guest—the fact that they were so rich they could support their son *carte blanche*.

When the partygoers and the caterers left, my mother pulled me aside, "Gail, ask Zach to go for a walk. You have to find out what is bothering him. He looks so unhappy, I can't bear it."

Mother wanted to know what was bothering him, so she asked me? I thought this to be a strange request, since Zach never talked to me. Our mother used me as her go-between to get information from other people. Perhaps she had forgotten the dynamic Zach and I shared which could be summed up as, "Never speaking to each other." Nevertheless, I complied.

"Zach, the party was nice, don't you think? Care to go for a walk around the lake? I think we both could use a little exercise."

"OK," was his quick response, which shocked me.

When we had walked for a few minutes and were away from the house, Zach opened up. "I feel trapped," he began, as he pulled a weed from the roadside and shredded it. "I feel like a mouse circling around my wheel in a cage. I am going to be working for the rest of my life."

I looked at him and did not know what to say, so I stayed quiet and pulled a weed myself. We walked in silence for a while and then he started talking again.

"I am never going to make enough money to satisfy Lennox," he blurted out. "If it were not for Mom and Dad, I don't know what would have happened to me."

He stopped talking and looked out onto the small lake, took a deep breath, and said almost with a hopeful quality, "I feel like I am going to die young."

He spoke but never looked at me. It was as though I was not there. Yet, he needed to hear himself talk, with me as his invisible sounding board.

I listened to this story and did not know how to respond. Zach, who had never worked aside from his medical training, felt trapped in a profession that would give him lifelong security and respect? I just did not get it.

When Zach stopped talking, I realized it was my time to respond. Speaking gently to Zach, in my new position as an advisor, I offered,

"You are so smart, everything will work out perfectly for you. You know Mom and Dad adore you and will do anything you want to make sure you are comfortable."

With that said, Zach turned to stare at me with cold blue eyes, and in that instant, he realized who he was talking to. With a smirk on his lips he turned around, never looking back, and walked home in a hurry.

That evening, Zach, Lennox, and Peter drove back to Chicago in Zach's new car. Our parents thought they had made a successful party. Zach received many lovely gifts and their guests all seemed pleased with the day.

With the gift that our parents bestowed, Lennox chose Maine. It seemed like an odd choice for two people so besotted with luxury.

In our car driving home, I told Russ about Zach's comments. This day was upsetting for me on many levels, one being it was our twelfth wedding anniversary. I thought for sure my mother would have at least mentioned it at the party and perhaps had a cake. Also, I was again hit in the face with the knowledge of the disparity between how Zach and I were treated. I learned he was gifted a large weekly allowance. My mother's sister Sara Lee—the one with the nose for good gossip—felt compelled at this party to enlighten me on how Zach and I were treated. Sara Lee told me how extensively Zach was being subsidized. She told me our parents were paying off Lennox's total debt which came to over two-hundred-thousand dollars. This was while both Russ and I were working for my parents and living paycheck to paycheck. It was so unfair!

At the time, Russ was going to school to get his MBA. He wanted to prove to my father that he was an asset to his uniform business. Russ studied hard and kept up with the latest news. When Russ heard where Lennox chose to go on their trip, he told me about an article he read in the *Wall Street Journal* regarding plastic surgery and breast implants. The article was about how doctors were setting up medical resorts so clients could have their surgery done without anyone else knowing. The recommended resort at this time was located in Maine. Clients of this medical resort would go for two or three weeks and come back completely healed from whatever procedure they had chosen. No one would be the wiser. Lennox returned with a new bra size of 36C.

This discovery inspired Russ to stay on top of the kind of news that would eventually help him chronicle many of Lennox's actions and decisions. Yet, when we told our family and friends, no one believed us. We lacked credibility, while she was always one step ahead.

Chapter Ten
THE LOAN SHARK

A government that robs Peter to pay Paul can always depend on the support of Paul.

— GEORGE BERNARD SHAW

Our parents used their wealth to bind us to them through gifts of their choosing.

"Don't worry, when we die, you will be very rich," Mother reminded us with a comforting smile and a little flip of her hand.

She used this phrase like a fortune teller seeing into our future. When Lennox heard Mother say this, her lips curled and her eyes appeared colder than usual. In that instant, our family dynamic became clearer to her which was Zach and I were faithful children programmed to wait for our coming windfall.

Our parents never told Zach how much money he had to live on therefore, he spent freely plus he received modest earnings from his young medical practice. Lennox watched the interplay between Zach and his parents when he needed something more. She understood how Zach played them and soon she would have them in the palm of her hand as well.

Lennox was accustomed to shopping in the most exclusive stores in Toronto. She knew how to dress to impress and her closet was filled with the work of high-end designers. She moved with an entitlement that I had only seen in powerful people. She walked with great purpose, but never fast. The jewelry she purchased came with a story, much like good art. She knew to feature only one stunning piece at a time.

Lennox enjoyed shopping at the designer boutiques on Chicago's Oak Street. She enjoyed telling me how she drew attention from other shoppers.

"Yes, I was shopping today on Oak. People kept stopping me on the street. They all think I am a celebrity and inquire which stores I frequent. Whenever I enter a store here, the clerks greet me and offer refreshments. I am on their list of preferred clients."

Mother could not understand how Lennox, a girl from a poor family, had so much pizzazz. She marveled whenever she saw her daughter-in-law; her manner of dress was something she wanted to emulate. Lennox's clothes were unique *haute couture*, and tailored to fit perfectly. Mother, always curious about her daughter-in-law, used me to glean information. But she didn't like the news I gave her regarding Lennox's lavish spending.

"Gail, you do not understand fashion at all. Really, you are one to talk. I am going to ask Lennox if she will take you shopping. You really need help."

What a contrast I was to Lennox. I never had the *chutzpah* (audacity) to shop as Lennox did, plus my parents were not subsidizing me.

In the 80s, credit cards were being issued. Credit card companies solicited people by phone, and sent mailers offering potential customers a variety of deals. One day a clerk at one of the boutiques asked Lennox if she knew about them. She explained to her it would make shopping easier not having to carry a checkbook around. Lennox had no credit history, so she used Zach's name and credentials to apply for their first card and then applied to receive all of them. She charged on one until she reached her credit limit and then rolled the balance over to a new card.

She wasn't alone in this creative spending style—it was coined the

Domino Effect. The two lovebirds thought they were so clever, even bragging about this system to Russ and me. But then the day came where there were no new cards to pass the debt on to. One after another the companies cut off her credit and demanded payment. She realized it was time to inform Zach of their problem.

My girlfriend Kay told me this story. Her boyfriend Ryan, at the time, was friends with Zach and that is how she learned the details.

"Gail, your sister-in-law knows how to manipulate your brother. Did you know that they are in debt?"

"No, my mother never tells me anything negative regarding Zach. How much debt?" I was thinking of my father and felt he would explode when he heard this story.

"Well, Ryan told me that Lennox asked Zach if they could drive to Wisconsin. You know how Zach is never fully present when he is driving. When we have been driving with him, he becomes so engrossed in his music or the conversation that he forgets where he is going. Therefore, Lennox used this opportunity to ask him if he would like to take her to the country for the weekend. She tells me your parents' home is beautiful. You really should invite us."

I must be an easy mark. I of course agreed, if only to hear the rest of her story.

"Well, Zach told Ryan he loved to take trips with her because when they were in the car together, they discussed the latest cultural and news events. But once in the car, Lennox was quiet. He understands now that she was using the time to gage his mood and was figuring out how to approach him with their credit problem. Zach asked her what was wrong and if she was unhappy. She told him she was happy but that it was hard for her to stay home all day waiting for him to return from the hospital. Then she complained about the one-bedroom apartment saying the space confines her."

"Zach was shocked and he asked her, "What do you mean, 'stay home'? You work out, you go out shopping, and we go out for dinner every night. I thought you had a daily routine you enjoyed. Then he asked her what was really wrong."

"And she told him that she does not have enough money to maintain the lifestyle that she had when she was married to Steven. She reminded him how much she likes to shop and how she paid by using credit cards. She told him the credit card companies wanted payment and she has been receiving many calls from bill collectors. Then she suggested asking your parents to pay off the credit card balances."

As my friend was telling me this story, everything was falling into place, just like dominos. I listened to my parents' conversations whenever I drove them. My mother was always commenting on Lennox's wardrobe and the couple's choice of five-star restaurants. Dad would look down at his hands with a little tight smile on his face but never say a word. And I was always wondering how Zach could afford his lifestyle. I knew that he never paid attention to his bank balance. He just wrote checks knowing Dad took care of everything for him.

Kay continued, "Lennox explained her plan to Zach. She located a moneylender."

I stopped Kay, "What! Are you talking about a gangster?"

"Yes," Kay gave a little girly giggle, "The girl at one of the boutiques told her about a man who would give them cash right away. She made an appointment with him. I believe Ryan told me they are meeting with him this week. Zach told Ryan he thought this experience would be fun. He wondered if the moneylender delivered the cash or if they needed to go to a dark alley like he envisioned from the movies he had seen. He felt Lennox is realistic and a smart thinker. He laughed as he told Ryan that life with her was an adventure."

"Zach told Ryan that Lennox had organized a meeting with Joey, the moneylender, at an Italian restaurant in Cicero tomorrow night. They have to bring him a recommendation from two friends, Ryan is writing his up today and they need to bring proof that they own their car and have other assets. Zach told Ryan it will be just like going to a bank, only quicker because Joey can make a decision on the spot. He will give them cash upon approval of their application and interview."

I knew the area called Cicero. It was primarily a manufacturing town served by several railroads and was once home to Czech immigrants. I read enough gangster novels to understand that in Cicero, there was a black-market economy called "you name it." It was known as a tough neighborhood because Al Capone used to live there. This was during the 20s and prohibition. I believed it still was the headquarters for the mob. I wondered how Zach, my elitist brother, would respond to this type of community. I was sure this was a place in Chicago he had just read about.

All heads turned when Lennox, wearing one of her Chanel dresses, and Zach dressed in his traditional plaid jacket with complementary ascot, entered. They looked so out of place in this working man's neighborhood where the clientele dressed in work clothes reflective of their blue-collar jobs. The men sitting at the bar looked as though they just finished their eight-hour shift and were having a cold beer before heading home to their families. They wore coveralls, soiled shirts, and steel toed work boots. Zach smiled to himself as he looked at the room, to him it looked like a theater set.

As they entered the dark smoke-filled room, they saw a traditional wooden bar, lined with tall dingy bar stools. The liquor bottles were displayed on a lighted cracked mirrored wall along with foggy hanging bar glasses. The beer tap handles reflected the types of beer that the clientele enjoyed. Nothing was imported. They went up to the bartender to ask where they could find Joey. The bartender pointed to the back of the building.

There was a traditional Italian neighborhood restaurant behind the bar. The tables all had red and white checkered tablecloths, accented in the center with basket weave straw style Chianti bottles, each stuffed with colorful tapered candles with the wax flowing down. They saw Joey sitting at a back table doing business with a Hispanic man. There were other people sitting at nearby tables waiting to talk to him as well. A young man approached them, and they told him they had an appointment to speak with his boss. The young man, Vince, told them to get a beer, they would have to wait.

Joey was a small man, dressed in a white shirt with sleeves rolled up and dark pants. He had no hair on his head and a huge cigar in his mouth.

"So, you must be Lennox," Joey looked her up and down with a smile on his lips as he joined them at their table.

"Yes, I was told you were a looker. Did you bring everything I asked for? You do understand the condition of this loan. It is only for one month and I charge fifteen percent interest."

Zach agreed to the terms and verbally committed himself. There was no paperwork to sign. Doing business with Joey, your word is your bond. Joey left them to finish their drinks and Vince returned with the cash. They had done it!

"Let's get out of here," Zach proclaimed.

Suddenly, he felt out of place with the people around him and was slightly afraid the money may be stolen before he reached their car. He was extremely nervous and began to sweat heavily after placing the cash in Lennox's large bag. When the deadline on the loan was coming close, Joey's colleagues started to call to remind Zach of his obligation.

"Zach, I am a friend of Joey's. He asked me to call you. He wants to know when you will be repaying your loan. It's due this week. You know, if he is disappointed we will be visiting you."

"Please, can you ask Joey if we can have another month? My wife is expecting her funds to come in any day now," Zach pleaded. Lennox told him her ex-husband was going to pay off their debt.

"Sure, we will talk to Joey," his associate replied, "but if he has to wait another month, the interest will be twenty percent."

At the end of the second month they still had no money to repay the loan. Joey's friends became threatening, calling Zach at work and giving him ultimatums.

"We know you are a doctor and you need the use of your hands. You either pay up by Friday or we are going to break some of your fingers to start. The longer it takes to pay the more pain you will feel." Zach realized he had to tell his parents. Lennox called Mother to invite them to dinner.

"Hello Mother dear," Lennox cooed with her strongest British accent, "Zach and I were wondering if you could have dinner with us tonight. We just heard about a darling restaurant near your flat."

Mother was happy the young couple wanted to have dinner with them. They had not seen them for a couple of weeks. "Of course Lennox," she gushed, so grateful for a phone call from her daughter-in-law.

After they decided on the time, she went promptly to her closet to check out her wardrobe. Zach and Lennox went to first-class restaurants in the city, so she wanted to look young and fresh.

Lennox chose Hugo's on Rush Street. Because of her connections with the clerks at the boutiques, she was able to get a reservation. That night, Zach and Lennox went to pick up our parents. When Mother told me about her evening, this was the first part of her story which did not make sense to me. Zach never went out of his way to pick anyone up.

Zach wanted to please our parents and realized he needed to distract them from the question at hand. Therefore, he and Lennox went shopping, they both knew that dressing well was another enhancement. Zach appeared in a Ralph Lauren jacket with a matching tie and handkerchief. Lennox dressed in a beige couture suit from the 28th shop. As always, they made a stunning couple, just what his parents loved and now expected.

Zach and Lennox appeared so happy to see them, telling each of them how beautiful they looked, which was the right thing to say to our parents in order to get the evening moving along in the right direction.

Once they were seated in the quiet section of Hugo's, Lennox took over the ordering ritual. She understood her in-laws could not read a menu where everything had a fancy name with a special preparation and a high price tag.

"Good evening madam, can I offer you something to drink?" asked the elegant server dressed in black pants, white shirt, and black morning jacket.

"I will order for the table," Lennox responded to the server and took charge. My parents were impressed as they looked at each other and then smiled as they nodded their heads at their sophisticated couple.

"My husband and I will each have a scotch and water, dry, no ice, and my in-laws would like a diet coke and a root beer." As she ordered this, she looked away from them and gave the server a knowing smile.

"Then, we would like the house special appetizers for the table. Dr. Dale, Mrs. Dale, and I will have the fish special and Mr. Dale will have the New York strip steak, medium well with mashed potatoes and gravy."

With the ordering completed, Lennox settled down in her chair and looked out on the floor of the restaurant to see how many people were taking pleasure in her appearance.

Everyone enjoyed their meals. The service was impeccable. After dessert, Zach was given the go ahead from Lennox to start his plea.

"Mom, Dad, Lennox and I have a problem."

"Oh, no!" Mother exclaimed, although she was secretly happy because she loved to solve problems for her son.

"What's wrong?" she asked.

"Do you need money?" Dad asked, right to the point.

"I do, Dad." Zach blurted out, "My expenses have increased since Lennox came to live with me. I am grateful to you and Mom for my weekly allowance and I am still receiving a small salary from the hospital and my practice. But you do understand my practice is young and I have to acquire patients. I hope soon I will be able to earn more, and we will be self-sufficient."

"Yes, yes, Zach, Dad and I were wondering how you were managing," Mother replied with love in her eyes and her checkbook ready.

"Yes, well, uhm." Zach began again. He was trying to look as pathetic as he could so his parents would feel sorry for him.

"Lennox has had too much time on her hands. When she lived in Toronto, she was busy with the boys and the temple. But without her children she has been sad. Lennox wanted to make our life perfect. She likes to look nice for me."

"Yes," the parents nodded their heads in agreement, "Lennox is a beautiful woman."

"Oh, thank you," Lennox replied demurely, looking down at her lap with a roguish smile.

Zach took a swig of his second scotch and water and continued in a rush, "Well, her shopping has gotten a little out of control." And with a deep breath holding the hand of his loved one he told the truth, "We now owe eighty-five thousand dollars cash to a money lender. I was contacted today and told if I do not pay by the end of the week, they will start by cutting off my fingers or God knows what else," Zach tried to make light of the problem, so his parents would not be overwhelmed.

Our parents looked at their child with eyes of love and shock. They were not sure they heard correctly.

"What are you telling us Zach?" Mother asked almost blanching.

"What I am telling you is, if we do not pay by Friday, you may never see me whole again," Zach responded with desperation in his voice.

Our parents looked at each other in disbelief, yet their reaction was not one Zach nor Lennox could have ever expected. Instead of getting mad, they thought it was hysterically funny. They thought it was adorable and resourceful of Zach to find a moneylender. Even hearing the gangster's name set them in a laughing mood. How incredibly creative they believed Zach and Lennox to be. What a wonderful story to repeat to all their friends! They were anxious to meet Joey. They had heard of loan sharks, but now the opportunity to meet one was an adventure of a lifetime.

Mother spent the next day shopping for the perfect dress to wear to meet the moneylender. She felt she would have to present herself in good quality clothes. Her discount shirts and skirts would not work for this occasion. So, she went to Marshall Fields to shop the sale racks for designer bargains. She also went shopping for a large briefcase to put the money into because she was told Joey did not take checks.

Dad spent his time at the bank where he was friendly with the bank president. When he told the story of why he needed this much cash, he was told the bank did not keep that much on hand. The bank needed to have the money delivered. The bank president told Dad that he could have the cash in two days. But when my father explained it was a matter of life and death for his son, the banker got on the phone and worked some magic.

On Friday, with the payment encased in a briefcase as they had seen in the movies, Mother wearing her new outfit and Dad in one of his navy sports jackets, they took a cab to a well-known Italian restaurant on Franklin Street where Zach and Lennox were waiting for them already seated in one of the many small discrete rooms.

"We had such an interesting evening," Mother told her best girlfriend, Ester, the next day. "We met at a great Italian steakhouse, Gene and Georgettes. It was located underneath the elevated train line near the Merchandise Mart. It is an old-time steakhouse. The food was really expensive, David picked up the check. Have you ever eaten there, Ester? Zach told us it is frequented by politicians, celebrities, and gangsters," saying the last in a whisper and a slight giggle to her voice.

"Joey, the moneylender, was such an interesting man, he told great stories and we laughed a lot. You should have seen Zach and Lennox, they looked so beautiful! Lennox wore a teal-colored suit with matching shoes and a little fur stole. She had her hair up in a twist, with a small pillbox hat. I think she could out chic Jackie O. Zach wore one of his darling plaid jackets with an ascot and dark pants. I think Joey was impressed with how smart Zach is because during dinner, Joey asked him for medical advice.

After the dinner, our parents put terms on the couple. They were two-fold. First, Lennox was to surrender all her credit cards to them so that they could cut them in half. They had heard about this problem called the Domino Effect on television. The presenter had told their audience that cutting the cards in half was one of the best ways to stop the problem. However, our parents never followed up after dinner because the cards were still in Lennox's possession and she was free to use them again as the outstanding bills had been paid. Second, Lennox was to get a job.

I would hear my parents tell this story to many of their friends. I would also repeat this story to my friends, wondering, "Is this normal?"

Chapter Eleven
ONLY THE BEST FOR BEAUTY

Life isn't about finding yourself. Life is about creating yourself.

— GEORGE BERNARD SHAW

Lennox started working for a publishing company in their magazine section. Her stories about this job were vague. I knew my parents told her to get a job, but how she obtained this one was a mystery. She reported to us she was working as an editor. Then Zach told me she was a model for one of their ad campaigns. He showed me a smoky black and white perfume ad featuring a woman in profile holding up her hair. I did not recognize her.

One day, she announced to the family she was going to be on "Donahue." "Donahue" was one of the first talk shows on national television at the time, and was produced in Chicago. She told us one of the producers of the show had seen her in one of the magazine's ads and wanted to put her on the show as a model. She was going to have her legs waxed on national television. The show was on late afternoon and I went over to my parents' house to watch. There she was, on a massage bed having her legs waxed.

"Did you see me on "Donahue"? The cameramen could not get

enough of me. They wanted to do the entire segment about me. The producers wanted Donahue to ask me about how it felt, how long it took and how long it lasted, you know, various questions. It was so much fun. I am sure I will get more recognition from this." Lennox told my parents the next day.

No such thing happened, but she did land a new job as an executive secretary at a large brokerage and investment firm. The new position emboldened her to look for a larger apartment. One of the doormen in their building told her about a four-bedroom penthouse available on the forty-second floor that just went on the market.

Mother later told me the following story, "Lennox negotiated with the owner to let her and Zach rent with an option to buy once their condo was sold." Then she went on to describe the evening and how she perceived Lennox's intentions.

"I believe her next step was to convince Zach to move and then have your father and I buy it for them. The apartment is so beautiful and perfect for her children when they come to visit. I feel certain she felt we would give in." my mother's voice this morning sounded deflated, not with the usual movement of high pitch to modulated.

As was customary, Lennox invited her in-laws to dinner. Her plan was to meet at a nearby restaurant and then bring them back to the building to see the apartment. The sky would be clear that night, guaranteeing a thrilling view of the city. How could they refuse their son this fantastic space?

She moved with ease through the apartment showing them all the rooms and speaking with flushed excitement as she described all the changes that she was planning or had already made. Mother was thrilled with the apartment. Dad only had one question on his mind, "How much does this cost?" Lennox looked at Zach, but Zach just looked away.

Lennox plowed ahead with her appeal, "Mom, Dad, the owner and I settled on two hundred and fifty thousand. I already had it carpeted and painted. We agreed to pay rent until we sell the one-bedroom. What do you think?"

"I think you do not have any savings to even make a down payment on a mortgage. I just paid off the moneylender, purchased Zach's medical practice, and paid off your lawyer bills. What were you thinking?" Annoyed and angered, Mother told me Dad looked at her with wild eyes, took her arm, and marched out.

"Give Dad the evening to think about this," were Mother's parting words. But for the first time my father had the last word, "No, Ruth. There is nothing more to say."

Lennox and Zach moved into the penthouse after his one-bedroom was sold. Lennox used the money from the sale to pay down her new debt. Then she started to buy furniture with the help of a designer. Once again, their bills started to mount.

Six months later, the four met for dinner on the 95th floor of the John Hancock building. The purpose of this dinner was again to ask for money. Lennox asked for funds to travel to England.

Her father had called to say that her mother was dying and Lennox wanted to get back to England to see her one last time. Could they please help?

How could they refuse? Lennox left for England the next day, and returned two months later with the sad news that her mother had passed.

While she was gone, the owner of the condo called Dad at work while I was sitting in his office. When he hung up he was shaking his head, looking down at his hands, and breathing heavy. He told me Lennox and Zach had not paid the rent for the past four months. The reason she was calling Dad was that she could not get a hold of Lennox or Zach. Dad was not surprised. He paid the back rent on the condo and told Zach to prepare to move to an apartment building where he was a partner. There were many vacancies in this building, so he was able to get them a two-bedroom at a good rate.

When I talked to Mother about Zach's move, she told me about the conversation she had with Lennox that morning.

"Mom, you know we are moving into your rental building next week. But I have a problem with the number two." Lennox told Mother.

"What's wrong with the number two?" Mother asked, thinking Lennox was going to tell her a joke. "It's just for you and Zach. You won't be there forever. Just until Zach gets established."

"Well, you know the boys will be coming and there is no room for them. Then there is the issue of closet space, there is none! And of course, there is no washer/dryer in the unit. You cannot expect me to mix my laundry in with the horrible tenants you rent to, can you?"

Mother and Dad felt badly for Lennox, because she just lost her mother, so they gave in and knocked down a wall to the studio next door to make their space a three-bedroom.

Lennox had been a part of our family for seven years now and Mother still could not understand how she was able to purchase expensive new outfits. Every time they saw the couple, Lennox was dressed to the nines, never wearing anything twice. When Mother asked her about her expanding wardrobe, I watched as Lennox looked Mother directly in the eye, with a comfortable smile on her lips, and using her icy British accent explained,

"My boss sees me as a reflection of what his firm wants to project in wealth management. Therefore, he gives me an allowance to purchase clothes."

Mother bowed her head and accepted this explanation. She wanted to believe this could be true in the world of finance, so she let it go. It was a new world out there, corporations used their image to show prosperity and the old ways of doing business appeared to be fading.

When Dad, who admired jewelry, inquired about a diamond and ruby pin she had on, her story was so out of the ordinary, it had to be true.

"Oh, yes, this pin. Isn't it lovely? A client from our office presented it to me. He gave it to me because he thought I was extremely helpful. He needed to speak to my boss, Mr. Nero, and I was able to quickly get ahold of him. He thought I deserved something special for my efforts," Lennox explained.

Dad listened and tried to make her stories plausible. He spoke to Mother:

"I have seen this type of gift giving in the movies, Lennox does look like a movie star. People are always looking at her. I believe her boss's clients might be making a play for her. And Ruth, when you ask Zach, he never contradicts her stories."

They started to tell all their friends about how lucky Lennox was, hoping someone would give them insight into her life. Their friends, however, had no answers, they just enjoyed hearing the stories and were waiting for the next installment.

Soon, it seemed everyone Lennox met was handing over admiration gifts, even her poor father was sending her expensive presents.

"Yes," Lennox told them as they sat down to dinner at one of the new, wonderfully reviewed restaurants in the city,

"My father sent this to me today. It was my mother's and he insisted I have it."

Mother looked at the diamond and mother of pearl earrings her daughter-in-law was wearing and wondered.

"How can Lennox's father afford such expensive earrings for his wife? I understood he was a plumber."

Every new piece of jewelry had a story and Zach just sat there and listened but never interrupted his wife with questions or comments.

"David, what do you think Zach is thinking when he gets that faraway look every time Lennox tells us a story? Do you think Lennox is playing around with other men and these are the gifts she gets from them? How can Zach not be suspicious of where the jewelry and clothes comes from? Do you think he is so absorbed in his career that he is not paying attention to her? It seems to me that he and Lennox are leading separate lives. I am getting nervous."

One cold, miserable Chicago day, Lennox accompanied Zach to the Dale's 68th floor luxury condo. I was there when Mother opened the door to greet them, Lennox stood in the threshold looking stunning, wearing a full-length white mink fur coat. With her arm linked tightly to Zach's, Lennox looked up and smiled when Mother opened the door.

"Lennox, that is some coat!" Mother said as she looked her up and down to try to assess how much the coat was going to cost Dad.

"Where did you buy it? David, Gail, come here quickly, you have to see Lennox."

With sparkling eyes, and a huge smile on her face, she turned like a model on the runway, strutting down the hall and back. Our parents were laughing at how adorable they thought she was and they could hardly wait to hear how she was given this gift. They hoped Zach did not buy it because they were sure the coat was expensive. They guided the couple towards their formal living room and settled themselves on their yellow French Louis 14th sofa, motioning to Zach and Lennox to sit on the matching yellow side chairs.

"How many times do you think we have sat on this furniture in the past forty years?" Mother asked us with a laugh as we all turned to Lennox to hear her tale.

"You know, I just returned from Canada," she began. "Well, one day when I took the boys out for ice cream, Andy spilled chocolate sauce on my green wool overcoat, it was a bloody mess. I was upset but could not stay mad at my darling son. I tried to clean the coat the best I could, but the stain did not come out. I didn't want Andy to feel bad, therefore, in order to divert the boys, I took them all to a movie. When we came out of the theater, we walked toward the rental car. When Henry went to sit in the back seat, he saw a big wrapped box. The box was wrapped like a present with my favorite floral design paper and a huge yellow ribbon and bow. This white fur coat was in the box, but no note. The boys and I think it was a gift from their father. They think he might have followed us and saw that my coat was ruined. He is still in love with me, you know, and I think he wanted to make me happy."

"How can this not be true," we wondered after they left. Zach did not have the money to purchase a fur coat for Lennox. Therefore, this story must be true. My mother felt her son was trustworthy and ethical. Yet Zach never confirmed nor denied the authenticity of Lennox's stories. I watched him as Lennox spoke, he appeared rigid and his eyes had a hypnotized glassed over look. We were all afraid to confront him because we never wanted to upset the prince.

In June, Lennox was given an antique MG model-A convertible, from a complete stranger. The couple drove to Wisconsin to visit our parents at their summer home for the weekend in this car. When they pulled into the driveway, Russ and I were helping Dad outside washing Mother's Mercedes-Benz coupe. As we looked up from washing the car's tires, we saw the couple emerge laughing and tickling each other.

"Zach, Lennox, whose car is this? Did you rent it for the weekend? It looks old."

"No, Dad we didn't rent it. It's Lennox's. Is Mom home? We want to tell you the story."

When we all were seated in their screened-in porch facing the lake, I served lemonade as we waited to hear the story of the car.

"Isn't the car terrific! On Monday, when I was leaving work, I noticed stock certificates flying on the street around a parked car. I collected them, there must have been fifteen certificates from various New York Stock exchange companies. I tracked down the owner's phone number and called him. He was so grateful to me for collecting his stocks. He told me his son took his car and the stocks were sitting in the front seat in a folder. While his son was driving, he had opened the roof for fresh air. On departing the car, he placed the folder on the front seat and a gust of wind must have picked the certificates up as they were not fully secured."

"Then he told me, 'you really cannot count on spoiled children to handle important documents.'" As Lennox relaxed in her chair, she took a sip of the drink, nodded her head, and looked directly at me, "He was so grateful to me for calling and returning his stock certificates that he wanted to give me a gift. He told me the stocks were worth over two million dollars and if someone else had found them he would have had many problems. He is a collector of old classic cars and he gave this one to me as a reward. He presented this car to me yesterday. Isn't it adorable?"

My parents retold Lennox's latest story to all their friends. The more they told people about Lennox's good fortune, the more they got into her stories and found reasons to believe they were true. Perhaps a grateful rich eccentric man, who had many classic cars, would gift one in appreciation. Something like this has never happened to anyone else except to Lennox. Moreover, there was never a clue from Zach, since he never said anything. He sat in silence and looked at her with admiration. Our parents were so sure that if it were not true, Zach would correct her or at least call them later to elaborate.

Lennox loved to give gifts as well. She shopped at designer stores and purchased items for Mother, Aunt Sara Lee, and Aunt Bev–little Gucci scarves as dinner gifts, or Chanel No.5 perfume, just because "I love you." All of her gifts expressed status through their unique design and markings. Our parents also enjoyed giving gifts. Theirs came from discount stores such as TJ Maxx or Marshalls or from bulk designer knockoffs purchased at the flea markets in Florida. Dad was especially fond of ten-dollar watches. Mother specialized in five-dollar pins full of fake stones.

One year, I hosted a Valentine's Day party. Russ and I were living in the northern suburb of Wilmette, in a distinctive prairie style home that Russ and I worked hard to maintain. This was going to be Lennox's first time meeting my friends and I planned many surprises to make the evening special.

The color scheme was red: small sparkling red hearts sprinkled on the pure white tablecloth, tall red tapers in the two three prong silver candlesticks, and a centerpiece bouquet of long-stemmed red roses in a red crystal vase. Our menu was spaghetti with marinara sauce for the main dish and a red velvet cake for dessert.

I had also determined a dress code. The ladies all arrived in simple combinations of red and white blouses and skirts. The men sported white shirts with red ties. Everyone was talking and having cocktails when my brother and Lennox made their customary late arrival. Zach wore a deep red velvet smoking jacket and plaid pants. On his head was a red beret with a small red plume and he was smoking a large carved pipe. Lennox entered wearing a red satin strapless gown with a huge red feather plume in her pulled-up hair. She was carrying an exquisite basket filled with dark chocolates for each of my guests. The couple quickly became the center of attention.

"Oh Gail, your sister-in-law is amazing. Would you mind if I made dinner plans with her and Zach without you?" one of my neighbors asked.

"No, go right ahead Beth," I replied, as I made a mental note to never speak to her again.

The evening was wonderful on the surface, but I was so mad I was seeing red! I had hoped to introduce Lennox to my friends in an informal setting. But true to her character, she had to be the center of attention. I knew we could never be friends because she always made me feel as though I needed to compete with her, but I knew I was no match.

I called my mother the next day at eight-thirty.

"Mom, can you believe Lennox? Why would she do that?" I was hoping for compassion.

"What do you mean? She made your party a success. What are you complaining about?"

"Well, she upstaged me in my own house. I think that is something to be pissed off about. Why don't you get it?"

Mother never got it. The party only cemented my dislike of my sister-in-law. Lennox could not just show up and mix with my friends, she had to stand out. Wherever she went, she made herself the focal point. Everyone remembered their interactions with her. She knew how to make a lasting impression. However, she never really spoke to anyone in depth. She never gave any of my friends more than five minutes of her attention. I felt she was a politician. Always asking questions but never listening to the answers.

Another issue I could never understand about her was her ability to connect with our family. While she was at work, she had time to call Mother and my aunts to make plans for the weekend or just to chat. She enjoyed telling the family about her and Zach's busy life, never asking about theirs. Her favorite person to call and torment was me.

"Hi, Gail," she would start, with a light, high pitch to her accent.

"I lost two more pounds. My trainer is working me really hard. I have a final fitting for a dress this afternoon. Zach and I are going to be sitting in box seats at the opera with one of his patients. Oh, look at the time. I've got to go."

Chapter Twelve
LIFE CAN CHANGE IN AN INSTANT

Be yourself, everyone else is taken.

— OSCAR WILDE

By 1988, Lennox had been working for two years in the fast-paced world of finance at a prestigious brokerage and asset management firm in Chicago. She was the executive assistant to the executive vice president of the main downtown office. It was the time of junk bonds and corporate raiders who would buy up undervalued corporations and split them up. The company she represented was a lead broker firm in many of these transactions. The firm relied on their brokers' contacts to move their product into their customers' portfolios while maintaining special client relationships.

Lennox's chief responsibility was client relations. She called the firm's high-rolling clients and offered them complimentary tickets to cultural and sporting events in the Chicago area. Some of the tickets were to prestigious sky boxes for the Cubs, the White Sox, the Bulls, the Bears, or the Blackhawks. Likewise, the firm sought out corporate sponsorships at cultural institutions such as the Art Institute of

Chicago, the Lyric Opera, or the Chicago Symphony Orchestra. She courted special clients with regular offers to attend these events.

The clients enjoyed talking to Lennox, and with her charm and aristocratic tone, she won them over. She also had a good memory and was able to recall the details they told her about their lives, such as their wife's name, the ages of their children, or their favorite activities. She excelled at sending them notes or presents on birthdays, anniversaries, or other important events in their lives. She easily proved her worth and was given expanded duties within the year.

With her position at this firm, she landed premium tickets to hard-to-get shows and performances. And she was generous, she took Mom and Dad to the Lyric Opera to see Madam Butterfly and graced Russ and me with football tickets for our son's ninth birthday. When we arrived at the plush suite, there were team jerseys on the chairs for my children and their friends.

I wasn't used to lavish accommodations and I felt like we were stealing. Russ had to remind me that this is how brokerage business for wealthy clients was done.

Soon Lennox was traveling regularly to New York, Washington DC, and California. She continued to project an aura of sophistication combined with mystery. Approaching her fortieth birthday, Lennox decided to give herself a party. I thought she wanted a big birthday celebration to take the edge off that milestone number, but I was wrong. This party was the herald of a revelation that changed the course of my family forever.

The official invitation arrived by special messenger. The messenger was dressed as a minstrel singer; he handed me a golden scroll that was embossed in gold letters and had golden tassels on the ends. It was printed on the finest paper I had ever touched. It also came with a map. It read:

The Master of the Household is Commanded by
Dr. & Mrs. Z. Dale
To invite Mr. and Mrs. Klein
to an English Day in The Country
Cocktails and Luncheon will be served

July 2, 1988, at 1:00 o'clock

On the day of the party the temperature in Chicago was approaching one hundred degrees. Russ and I put our children in the car and headed out, map in hand. We soon found ourselves at the Cook County Forest Preserve near Morton Grove. Once we turned into the preserve, there were signs with flags everywhere showing us the way. The flags were of the United States, Britain, Canada, and Scotland, each representing a phase of Lennox's life.

We parked our car in the nearby field and walked down a path through the lush foliage. Finally, we arrived at a huge white medieval tent. I thought we had entered another world.

"Russ, we are not dressed correctly. Lennox told me to dress like we were going to the lake house on a summer day, very casual. Look at her guests! They are all dressed as though they are attending an English horse race. Where did the girls find those floral dresses with huge hats? Do you think Zach supplied his friends with his collection of plaid jackets? Ugh, I had no idea this was going to be such a dressy affair. Where is my mother? Wait, I see my cousin Diane and her family. Thank God, they look like us." In that moment I realized that Lennox had managed to have the Dale family dress as her poor American relations to have us stand out.

It was so hot that we decided to go into the tent which was air-conditioned. When we pulled the plastic covering open we saw the tent floor was lined with hardwood laid down for dancing. There were around fifteen round tables for eight covered with Laura Ashley tablecloths. Each table was accented with beautiful vases filled with summer flowers. I noticed five huge ice sculptures, one was of a mermaid, others were a dragon, a swan, a dog, and an eagle. These fantastic pieces of ice were sweating in the air-conditioned tent. A ten-piece orchestra was playing Broadway show tunes and many of the guests were dancing. The waiters wore black tuxedos and the waitresses wore black skirts with white shirts and starched white aprons. All the serving staff wore white gloves as they roamed the crowd offering an assortment of *hors d'oeuvres*. Three bartenders prepared mixed drinks and poured vintage wines. Lennox hired a primly uniformed nanny for the day to help the children search for four hundred dollars' worth of quarters hidden in a sandbox built for the occasion. Everywhere we looked there was over-the-top opulence.

Russ and I walked up to various people to introduce ourselves, but we were never able to click with Zach's friends. The conversation started and ended with, "It is so hot," and another comment from someone else, "This is an incredible party!" and then inevitably they waved at their friends walking by and excused themselves.

Lennox's youngest sister, Anna, came from England with her husband, her two young children, and her father, Peter, who was still dressed in the same fashion that we last saw him, a dark gray suit and white shirt. It seemed to me that he came to every gathering holding his signature glass of scotch and large unlit cigar. The middle sister, Karson, came in from Toronto with her husband and brought Lennox's three boys.

At the time of this party, Zach and Lennox had been together for eight years. I had heard about her sisters and I was anxious to meet them. When I saw her family standing to the side of the tent, I walked over to introduce myself. However, when I went up to them, they turned their backs to me. As they averted their faces, I thought I detected a sneer.

"Russ, what did I do wrong? Is it because of how I am dressed?"

When the party was over and we were driving home, I thought to myself that I should have listened to the little voice that plays all the time in my head and tried to talk to her sisters, I could have asked them about Lennox. My parents had impressed on me that I ask inappropriate questions, that I am blunt, and impatient. Knowing this, I walked away. Perhaps I really did not have the energy for confrontation and did not want to start a fight with them that I knew I would never win.

As the party progressed, it felt as though the two families were in separate camps. I went up to Mother to ask her what she thought of this affair.

"Mom, can you believe this party? Have you spoken to Zach? Did he put this together?"

She responded in a way that told me her mind was somewhere else,

"You know, your father's best quality is that he is an ethical man. He would never do anything to harm anyone, plus he is honest, so is your brother, Zach is the second-best man I know." My mom gave me this speech regularly when she wanted to keep me quiet and put me down. She never answered my question.

Zach and Lennox came late to their own party, dressed spectacularly in white. When they entered I watched as they swooped in holding hands, gliding royally through the party, talking and laughing with all their guests.

Lennox cooed as she welcomed each of her guests with an embrace.

"I am so glad you were able to come!"

"Did you have a hard time finding this spot?"

"Are you having a good time?"

"Yes, it is very hot, so please enjoy a cool drink."

"I am going to introduce you to my…"

"My family came in from England and Toronto for this day, isn't it lovely?"

"Aren't my sister's two children darlings?"

"Oh, yes, those are my boys," she said as she pointed with her manicured finger towards her sons, who were groomed better than everyone there except for her and Zach. Each one handsomer than the other but looking nothing alike. The eldest, Jordan, thirteen, was tall and thin with thick dark hair and blue eyes the same color as his mother's. Henry, eleven, had curly brown hair, brown eyes, and was short. Andy, nine, had blonde hair, green eyes, and a full face. She dressed her sons in plaid shorts and polo shirts. Each wore a different color pair of Keds to offset their shirts. They appeared to have stepped out of a fashion magazine. Lennox also dressed her sister's children. Her nephew was eight and she dressed him like her sons, and the little girl was six and wore a floral dress that matched the table cloths and sparkling silver shoes.

About an hour into the party three troubadours appeared playing a Scottish tune and ushered us to sit down in the tent for dinner. Russ and I felt as if we were in a dream. We located our assigned seats and waited to be called to the buffet. The party was being catered by the best known restaurant in Chicago and everyone was anxious to try the food.

"Russ, another amazing party. Do you think my parents are paying for this one too?"

Russ just nodded his head and smiled, "Look, Lennox is getting up to speak."

I looked to Mother, who was staring straight ahead at Lennox, her eyes wide and her mouth in a tight smile. I could feel the tension in the tent as Lennox beckoned Zach to join her at the microphone.

"I want you all to know how happy Zach and I are to have you here for my fortieth birthday. I am also happy that my family was able to come today from England and Canada to help me celebrate. I would like to introduce my father, Peter, and my two sisters, their husbands, my niece and nephew, and my three gorgeous sons, of whom I am so very proud. I hope you all are enjoying yourselves. And remember, after lunch, we are inviting you to play cricket with my brother-in-law." Lennox proclaimed, followed by the crowd's laugh and a huge round of applause.

With this said, Lennox turned towards the door and a huge three-layer birthday cake rolled in and the orchestra played "Happy Birthday" and then "God Save the Queen." We all lined up for our piece of chocolate cake and a gift imported from England to take home. Mine was a bar of scented soap. Russ and I drove home from this amazing party and wondered for the hundredth time how Zach and Lennox could afford this type of lifestyle. The answer came the next day.

When I called my brother to tell him how much we enjoyed the event, he was bursting with his news.

"Gail, the party was not only in celebration of Lennox turning forty," he stopped speaking for a moment and caught his breath. "This is so crazy. Wait till I tell you. She is now able to come into her inheritance. After forty years, she can now disclose who she really is."

"What inheritance? Who is she?" I asked.

"Lennox is really the illegitimate daughter of the Duke of Northumberland."

"OK," I replied, not fully grasping anything he just told me, but homing in on the word illegitimate.

"Well," he continued in a rush, "Lennox just told me the story of her life. She was not sure the Duke would come through with her legacy, so she had never told me this story before. But now she can."

"Duke? You mean as in English nobility?" I asked.

"Yes, Lennox told me her mother worked for the Duke's family when she was a young girl. The young Lord fell in love with her. They had an affair and she became pregnant. The family married her off to Peter. The young Lord set aside money and a title for her because of his love for her mother. She was to receive her given legacy and title when she became twenty-one years old. The reason she did not receive it then was because she married a Jewish man. The Duke was displeased and withheld the inheritance until she turned forty, so now she can claim her title."

As Zach told me the story, I listened in detached disbelief and thought how strange that she married another Jewish man and she is now getting a long overdue title.

"She didn't want to say anything until she received the documents to prove her lineage. You should see these documents. They look so medieval. The stamps and the paper are incredible."

"Oh, and what is her title?" I inquired, channeling my mother. After all, this did sound like a whopper.

"She is the Lady Bristol. She owns one thousand acres of prime land in England and Scotland. She also owns a village which will pay her rent, providing her an income for life. The Duke included Lennox in his will, so she now has a part of his estate called Hartington Castle. She was given one fourth of this castle; the other three-fourths will be occupied by his other three legitimate children. We will be going to Scotland frequently now to take care of the property."

Zach told me all this in a voice of excited bewilderment. All his life he had loved the English style. In high school, before the Beatles made the English style of speaking cool, my brother spoke with an English accent. He loved British literature, history, culture, and the clothing that the aristocracy wore. The fact Lennox was from Britain, now owned land in Scotland, and revealed she was a noble—with the papers to prove it—fulfilled all my brother's dreams. He had won the marriage lottery.

I was as confused as he was excited. Zach accepted this story as absolute truth, and how could I doubt him?

That evening, I told Russ what Zach had told me and he showed me a *Wall Street Journal* article on how British and Scottish nobility were selling titles in England to Americans. The British government had stripped these families of their annual stipends but was allowing them to keep their titles, which were tied to the land. They were authorized to sell small plots of land containing royal titles and turning their properties into tourist attractions similar to American bed and breakfasts.

Chapter Thirteen
ENGLISH NOBILITY

The truth is rarely pure and never simple.

— OSCAR WILDE

Mother's life had centered on her prince, Zach, but now she switched her allegiance to his titled wife, Lady Bristol. The Lady gave her a glimpse of royalty, which set her apart from her friends, who bragged about their doctor or lawyer children, who of course were doing fabulously. Suddenly, Mother's friends were calling with questions about this new dimension to Lennox's life.

"Ruth, how did Zach not know she was a noble?"

That was the main question. Before, they merely asked, "Ruth, how could she have walked out on her three young children?"

No one could get enough of this strange turn of events, and they wanted to know what this new future would hold. The story became more than a mere curiosity, it became our family's fairy tale. After all, it's not what you ever expected growing up in a sheltered Jewish suburb.

"Yes, it's true," Mother told her girlfriends one by one. She never got tired of reporting the story she had heard from her son and doing a little embellishing of her own.

"Lennox is English nobility. The party she had at the forest preserves was not only to celebrate her fortieth birthday, but about receiving her inheritance. She told us she could not announce it that day because she had not received the last of her official paperwork. She wanted to be sure, and now it is official."

Mother was proud and excited, "Can you imagine, Ester, Zach has achieved his dream. Remember how he wanted to be English? I am so happy for him."

As time went on, the couple went to England for two weeks every other month. Lennox took a leave of absence from her firm and Zach took time off from his new medical practice. Mother told me Zach was leaving for England over the Thanksgiving holiday, so I had to ask, "Mom, how can Zach leave his practice for weeks at a time? Dad tells me a boss must watch his business. How can Zach watch his if he is traveling to England?"

"Zach has partners, Gail," Mother reminded me, "He is probably going to become the doctor to the royal family."

When I asked Lady Bristol about their travel plans, her explanation was, "I must be in Scotland over your Thanksgiving holiday. I now have many obligations. Next week, I need to be at a ribbon-cutting event. It's called, *The Festival of the Sheep.*" She gave me an uppity nod and walked away.

Lennox's full title was *Lady Bristol of Northumberland*, and in her presence, we were to address her as Lady Bristol. With this adjustment also came a subtler change to her appearance. Her hair became redder and thicker with the addition of more fillers. Her enhanced eyelashes were applied one-by-one and made of mink. She was more tanned, thanks to the tanning bed she never admitted to owning. And her rouge became more pronounced, giving her a dewy complexion, or a greasy one depending on the light.

Lady Bristol no longer shopped in boutiques, her clothes were designed especially for her in France and England by top designers. When she spoke, her accent was stronger and her conversation peppered with many "darlings" and other British inflections.

While Lennox was in Scotland, our parents had more time to spend with Zach. He even visited us at Dale Uniforms and joined us next door for lunch at Kepper's Deli—the type of restaurant the Lady would never be seen in.

"Have you heard from Lennox? How are her boys?" Mother inquired.

"Yes, Mother, she calls me every day. She says she is going to be coming home around Mother's Day," Zach replied as he patted our mother's hand.

Looking up, he flashed her his all-American smile—the one that said, "Aren't I precious?"

Mother could not believe how adorable and clever he turned out to be. "Oh, are her boys coming to Chicago?"

"Yes," he replied, "and she has a surprise prepared."

"Really?" Mother loved surprises but could never wait to find out what they were.

"No, no, you have to wait. Lennox is preparing something special and I know she wants to tell you herself."

Zach loved the way Mother adored Lennox. It pleased him to feel his mother's total acceptance and admiration for his wife.

Dad and I could see this secret was going to drive Mother to abstraction. Dad felt the return of a familiar feeling of dread, of having to write yet one more check to extract them from some harebrained scheme. Mother's fear was that Zach would be moving to Scotland. But her darling son was earnest and would not betray Lennox's command of silence, so she just had to wait.

Zach called Mother the following week to tell her Lennox called and asked if she could do the Lady a favor. "You know, before Lennox left for England, we joined the East Bank Club. She wants everyone to come to Mother's Day brunch there. It's our treat. She has some wonderful news we want to share. Could you call and invite the entire family, and of course Aunt Sara Lee and Barney?"

Knowing what her next question would be, he quickly offered, "Oh, yes, the boys are going to be there too."

On Mother's Day, true to her word, Lennox prepared a beautiful party at the fashionable East Bank Club in Chicago. It was a tradition for our family to get together at Aunt Bev and Uncle Irv's or at my suburban home, therefore it was a real treat to be invited out. The Dale family arrived at the designated time and was seated at two large tables towards the back of the room. True to form, our noble hosts, along with the Lady's three children, made their appearance an hour later.

Their entrance was of course, spectacular. The boys were dressed in powder blue seersucker suits, and glowed with shining clean faces and groomed hair. They took their places at the children's table and sat down sitting imperially straight in their chairs.

Zach and Lennox made their entrance next, waltzing through the restaurant in light blue summer suits. Zach sporting a yellow corsage in his lapel and Lennox wearing a huge summer hat with a colorful yellow feather pinned to the side. I could see that they had commanded the whole room's attention.

"Oh, darlings, don't you look wonderful," Lennox told the aunts and uncles as she hugged and kissed each one.

Everyone gradually made their way up to the opulent buffet, some of them lingering at the immense desert table groaning with cakes, pies, tarts, and an ice cream bar. But some of us could hardly eat because of the suspense over Lennox's big announcement.

I knew Mother was worried, and I knew Dad was counting everyone's drinks because he felt sure he was going to get stuck with the bill.

As usual, I was worried about how I looked compared to the rest of the room. And to make myself feel worse, when I looked over at the children's table, I noticed that Lennox's children knew the correct way to use cutlery, never spoke with their mouths full, and did not get up from their seats. They were so different from the children of the Dale clan, who acted like, well, *American children*. What a contrast in styles. Was I even getting the child-rearing part of life wrong?

I grumbled about this to my husband and felt like crying.

Russ just looked at me with loving eyes and said, "Their story is not over yet. Yes, they do have good table manners, and Lennox dressed them to look like men, but they don't seem happy. Didn't you notice how quiet they are? And Lennox has not gone up to them once since we sat down for the meal. They seem like accessories more than anything else."

Before Russ could continue, Lennox rose to make her long-awaited announcement. We were all on the edge of our respective seats as Zach stood to introduce the Lady,

"I want to thank everyone for coming today. It has been a long time since we have all been together," Zach declared as he sought out an approving glance from our mother. "Lennox, I mean Lady Bristol, has an announcement she wants to make and she wants everyone to hear it at the same time." He then moved aside and helped Lennox rise from her chair.

"I am so glad you were all able to come today to celebrate Mother's Day. I just returned from Scotland last week and then I flew to Toronto to get the boys," she said as she waved in her sons' direction. The boys smiled back.

"I have been rather busy, as I am sure you all know." at this point she looked down with a demure smile on her face and waited as an actress would for her next cue, Looking up at us to make sure we were all looking at her, she gave a little cough and continued, "As you may have heard, I am now to be addressed as Lady Bristol. Because of the legacy of my father, the Duke of Northumberland, I now own a castle in Scotland, as well as land with tenants." When she was sure she had our total attention, she turned her focus to her three sons.

"Thanks to the generosity of the Duke, my sons, upon their twenty-first birthday, will receive the title of Lord Bristol and be given a considerable amount of land in Scotland and England. The Duke has stated this in my *fiducie*. Their lives will be vastly different from what they know now."

With this part of her speech completed, I looked over at the tables filled with my family members to confirm that they too were in shock. I was wondering, what does she mean, "things are going to be vastly different?" Lennox kept talking but I missed some of the speech because I kept thinking about what this was going to mean our family.

"I will be spending more time in Scotland and so will Zach," she continued, opening her arms toward my parents and aunt. "I would like to extend a special invitation to my wonderful in-laws Ruth and

David, and Aunt Sara Lee and her husband Barney. I'd very much like them to come with Zach and me to England this summer as my guests."

Lennox stopped speaking and turned to face just my parents, Sara Lee, and Barney. "I want to show you the world Zach and I are now going to share," she proclaimed, with her hands clasped hopefully in front of her chest.

The family all looked to Zach, their blood relation and barometer of truth. He was beaming, so the family applauded the way people do in movies. The aunts got up to congratulate them and the cousins all talked among themselves. Our parents were in awe because they could not believe their good fortune. I looked to Russ, who just smiled and said, "Time will tell."

For the hundredth time, I rolled my eyes.

Lady Bristol and Zach were off to Scotland the next day. When they returned three weeks later, they organized a dinner for the soon to be travelers at the Pump Room in the Ambassador Hotel to talk about the upcoming trip.

Lennox and Zach showed them pictures of Hartington Castle. The discussion was mainly over travel dates. Dad was hesitant. He did not like to travel and he was uncomfortable in foreign settings.

"I will not take no for an answer," Lady Bristol told her in-laws. "I have made all the arrangements. Summer is the perfect time for you to come see our new home. You will be able to view the countryside at its best, with rolling green hills and lots of blooming flowers. It is so beautiful and enchanting."

At this point, Mother was fully under Lennox's—Lady Bristol's— spell. Other than a lingering concern over when the bill might come due, Dad only wanted what Mother wanted. And she really wanted to see the castle and to be with Zach, to experience his new world, where people dressed and acted like the people she'd seen in the movies. She wanted to feel rich and this was her chance. Lennox was going to show them a new reality.

With the invitation accepted, Mother went shopping in earnest. She wanted Zach to be proud of her and she wanted to prove to Lady Bristol that she too was chic. When Mother was not shopping, she was on the phone calling all her girlfriends to tell them about her forthcoming trip. No one tired of the still-unfolding story. Russ and I were never sure if anyone truly believed the tale of her son and his Lady, but Mother was undeterred. She promised her friends she would keep a journal so that they could share in her adventure.

These stories beat the real news of the world. Who else had a daughter-in-law who turned out to have such lineage? How would it all play out? The Lady's mystique was about to be tested.

Chapter Fourteen
THE INFAMOUS TRIP

The big question is whether you are going to be able to say a hearty yes to your adventure.

— JOSEPH CAMPBELL

On his morning call to our parents, Zach asked if he could have lunch with us at Kepper's Deli.

"Zach, I am so thrilled to see you!" our mother gushed as she rubbed his arm making sure he was really there.

"Well, Lennox wanted me to talk to you today."

"Oh, dear," Dad looked as though he was going to scream.

"No, Dad, we don't need any money, calm down. I wanted to meet with you today to discuss the trip. Now that Lennox has disclosed her true heritage, I must instruct you on your behavior towards her. Lennox, now Lady Bristol, wants to establish a protocol for the trip."

Zach, took a deep breath and looked out into space before he continued. We all sat straighter in our seats and bent towards him so that we would not miss a word of what he was going to explain.

"Listen, Lennox wants me to prepare you for the trip. She now requires you to address her in public as 'Lady Bristol' or use 'My Lady.'

When you talk about her to other people, you *must refer* to her as 'Lady Bristol' or 'The Lady.'" Zach spoke down to us as though we were now his knaves. His emphasis was on the word "her" which was coupled with the sincerest tone and body language.

Right away, Mother wanted to know if the men were to bow and the ladies were to curtsy. Zach eyes clouded over with the faraway stare that he had been perfecting since we were introduced to the Lady. The night before, Lennox, told him to be prepared for what his mother just asked. He couldn't believe Lennox understood his mother's thinking so well.

After Zach left us and I was driving them home, Mother went deep. "You know, David, we are experiencing something that we have no guidelines for. We really do not know how to act in our new roles as relatives to royalty. There are no television shows to guide us."

I felt that Lennox's ultimate plan in taking this group to England, was to impress on Zach how *gauche* our parents were. I was sure she felt deceived by their stories of great wealth that she had overheard at the condominium pool in Florida. Was she was out for revenge? I didn't tell Mother my thoughts; she wouldn't believe me anyway.

Lennox planned this trip to coincide with her forty-first birthday. Since my parents were given this gift on Mother's Day, Mother did not have much time to prepare. She now started to shop in earnest, after all, she always referred to herself as a black-belt shopper. Now was her chance to put that claim to the test because she desired to look as chic as the Lady. Her problem was that she only knew how to shop sale racks and discount stores.

"Gail, Zach and the Lady are leaving today," was Mother's opener on our eight-thirty phone call. "*The Lady*—will I ever get used to saying that?" She giggled. "Well, I am going to wear the gray suit with the pillbox hat on the plane to Heathrow. I know Sara Lee is going to wear her blue jean skirt and Burberry top. She wears the same things all the time. I hope the royal couple will be proud of us."

When my parents, aunt, and uncle returned home after their extraordinary three-week journey, Mother retreated to her summer home in Wisconsin and worked on her journal. She wanted to share her experience with all her friends and who knows, perhaps she could find a publisher.

She called her journal: *The Adventures of a Lifetime*. The problem that I saw as I read her fifty-five page epic, was that she appeared to be really interested in food. Every page was full of all the marvelous banquets Lennox organized for them. She described every morsel they tried which was strange to me because they were kosher eaters, never mixing meat with dairy. Yet on this trip, they must have forgotten the dietary laws of their Jewish faith. The other feature she wrote about at length was how they never saw Lennox during the day and all the fabulous outfits she wore at night for dinner.

Mother was enthralled with all the preparations Lennox planned for them. Every day they were taken by a chauffeur driven Land Rover or via the Highland Prince train to various locations in England and Scotland, always stopping to spend the night at castles or old inns. And Lennox paid for everything. Dad never had to pull out his wallet.

This was emphasized throughout her journal, the fact that Dad never had to pay. She also enjoyed adding little pejorative digs about her husband, informing her readers that he cried at night because he was nervous about the amount of money he watched being paid out. He was having a hard time changing the US dollar to British pounds and he had no idea what the price of anything was. His fears were mounting.

My mother wrote how Lennox seemed to glide through the trip, maintaining a flawless appearance even though she and her sister were starting to show wear and tear from the travel. The climax of the trip was the Lady's forty-first birthday party. The party was held in a castle owned by Lord and Lady Cuff. In her journal, she wrote that the staff was reminiscent of the television show "Downton Abbey" or "A Real Life: Upstairs and Downstairs." The travelers were in rapture. They were living their dream of being fabulously rich and pretending to have a long line of ancestors to back up their lineage. Mother's star struck feeling for her daughter-in-law was to continue forever. No matter what would happen in the future, both my parents were to be forever in her debt.

Chapter Fifteen
LASTING MEMORIES

> I've learned that people will forget what you said, people will forget what you did, but people will never forget how you made them feel.
>
> — MAYA ANGELOU

The three-week trip lasted forever in the memories of the four travelers. They glowed whenever they talked about their experiences in England and Scotland with Lady Bristol. The birthday celebration alone showed the grandeur of Lennox's new life, and she had it recorded on video tape as a parting gift to them.

"Yes, it is true. Lennox took us to the best hotels and some fabulous castles. We dined in royal palaces. Everyone we met knew the Lady, so we were treated like royalty ourselves." Mother kept retelling the story when she was with her friends. "Hatton Castle was where Lennox had her big birthday bash. There were bagpipes and Highland dancers performing for about forty guests. The castle was so romantic —can you imagine, fifty-two rooms? We had a hard time finding our way around. It was all very grand," said Mother, pausing briefly for effect. "It must have cost a fortune!"

Dad was quieter about the trip, perhaps because he was still mad about all the bills he had paid in the past. Mother looked over at her husband and elbowed him into smiling.

"David is always adding up costs. The entire time we were there, he tried to keep a running total of the day's expenses. But after the birthday party, he just gave up because he couldn't count that high without getting a tension headache." Dad just rolled his eyes.

Zach and the Lady kept up this fast-paced, expensive lifestyle. Lennox decided Chicago was too provincial for her and it was time to make their permanent home in her castle in Scotland. But first, she had to start working on Zach. She knew it was going to be hard to pull him away from his parents.

At this time, Zach was calling me on his car phone. We were not friends, but he liked to call me when he was driving, to pass the time to and from work. He enjoyed relating his stories about Lennox and his new life word for word to me just as our mother did.

"Gail, Lennox called me last night. We had a fun conversation. She told me she was having a wonderful time in England. She feels that the people who live there are more interesting. No one talks about money, they talk about theater, art, horses, and politics. And they have the funniest names, like Mr. and Mrs. Eatwell and Major Crapstone and his dah-ling friend Mrs. Tosh," Zach spoke in his snobbiest British accent. "Lennox wants us to move there. But I told her I don't know, I said let's just wait and see what happens this year. Do you think it would be hard to move all of our things to Scotland?" Zach asked me. One thing Lennox did not understand about the Dale men was their lack of adventure. Chicago, his parents, and his medical practice were Zach's anchor. It was going to take a lot to pull him away from it.

About two months later when he called me from his car, he had exciting news that he had a hard time explaining.

Speaking rapidly, he said, "Gail, Lennox just told me we are going to New York next month. I am going to receive a royal title. I am going to meet the Queen!"

"As in, you are going to meet *the Queen of England?*"

"Yes, Lennox has submitted a memorial to the Earl Marshal with the College of Arms. She lodged a memorial petition with them to have me titled. I cannot be titled as a Lord, Earl, Baron, or Duke, because I am not an English citizen. But I will be able to use the initials CBE after my name. Twice a year, the Queen honors a list of people to various orders of chivalry in the states. Commander of the Most Excellent Order of the British Empire gives me the honor of adding Commander of Medicine to my name."

"So, you are going to be titled by the Queen?" I repeated, aware that I was sounding like an echo.

"Yes, I have to be. It is not right for Lady Bristol to be introduced without her husband having a title. It sounds odd to be Lady Bristol and Dr. Dale. Lennox needs me to be titled to complete our crest."

"Ok, why do you need a crest? Are you thinking your crest is going to be similar to the one Dad had made to represent his uniform store?"

"No, this is a real royal crest—also called a badge. Then there is jewelry and other accessories." He loved to educate me on subjects where I was lacking. "This crest is needed for our coat of arms. We will have rings and seals made with this design. Even our cutlery will have a crest. Some other uses for the crest is for a heraldic standard. This is a narrow, tapering flag, a tradition in Scotland. When we are home, we will raise it letting our neighbors know we are in residence and they can visit. Lennox is already working on the design with the King of Arms. He is the one who approves the designs and grants permission to construct it. Her title gives her three parts to the crest and she needs me to make up the fourth. Mom and Dad said they will come with us next month. We are all going to meet the Queen!"

Our parents couldn't get enough play out of this story. "Yes, Lennox arranged for us to meet the Queen and see Zach titled. We are leaving next week. What do you think I should wear? I wonder if we will be given lessons on how to approach her. Can you believe this?"

But as the day neared, Lennox called Mother to tell her there was a change of plans.

"Oh Mom, I am so sorry to tell you this, but Zach's time slot to meet the Queen was taken away. An English actor replaced him. I know how badly you wanted to join us. A representative for the Queen will be presiding over the ceremony instead. I also learned you would not be allowed into the room because you are not British citizens."

"It was amazing," Zach told us when he called them from New York. "A representative of the Queen bestowed my title in a nondescript office building. I am really not sure where Lennox and I went, I am not familiar with Brooklyn. We had to wait in the hall for an hour, then we were taken into a small office. A man in a dark suit spoke to us for a while. He asked me some questions, it was all very official. Then he brought me into another small room that had many flags of England and Scotland. There, I had to kneel down on a low bench. He placed a sword over my head and spoke, just like you have seen in the movies when the queen knights someone. It happened so fast. We were given some official papers to sign, and that was it. I am now titled. We went to have our crest finished and ordered our rings, a seal, and standard."

When Zach returned home, he was wearing his own embroidered crest on his suit jacket and sporting a gold pinky ring with their coat of arms carved on its face. However, Lennox did not return to Chicago with him. She told him she had many duties to attend to in Scotland, another ribbon cutting for a new business and yet another farmer's cattle show to oversee.

A couple of days later, she was settled in a rental flat in Scotland and Mother told me about the call Zach received. Zach told Mother that Lennox was having a lot of fun. She met some Lords, and even a Duke. Zach told Mother that Lennox wanted him to move there permanently. Lennox assured Zach that she had enough funds for both of them to live on. Mother related this conversation to me with trepidation in her voice. Mother could not imagine her son leaving her to live in Scotland. Then to complete the story, Mother told me Zach's reply.

"Zach asked Lennox, about the Duke. He wanted to know if he was old and if he had a funny name. Lennox told him that they all have funny names. But no, he was not old. She had dinner with him last week. Actually, Zach told me the Duke took her to see a castle that is for sale called Tyninghame. She told Zach that it does not need as much work as Callay does. Remember I told you she sold Hartington Castle last year and purchased Callay. Now she told Zach that she is thinking of buying this other one. Zach is in shock and cannot believe she is going to purchase another castle. However, Lennox assured him that Tyinghame is in a better area. She was very excited about this castle. You know how adorable her voice becomes when she is excited. I love to hear her gush in her English accent when she is happy. Well, Zach told me Lennox was pressuring him to come and see it. But he told her he can't come for a while, he has a lot of patients to see. He asked her when she was planning on coming home." As Mother relayed this story to me, I could hear the fear in her voice. I wondered if she feared Zach leaving or Lennox having an affair with the Duke.

After eight days had past, she told me about her conversation with Zach the night before when we spoke during my eight-thirty slot.

"Gail, Lennox called him last night. She told him she had been busy and this was her first chance to return his calls. She was so excited because she had closed on Tyninghame Castle on Wednesday. She hired a castle designer to work on the remodeling. She told Zach it is a very old castle and no one has lived in it for generations. It has beautiful gardens and miles of untouched land. She signed off on all the improvements and now she is coming back to Chicago next week. She is planning on staying for the summer while the castle is being renovated. The boys are coming to Chicago with her and she is going to place them in summer camp during the day. Her father will also be coming to help with the boys. They will be flying in the next week."

What Lennox did not tell Zach, but we learned about later, was she had contacted the janitor in the building to see if there were any vacant apartments for her father and her boys to stay in for the summer months. In the past when her children came to Chicago, Mother called on Zach and Lennox's behalf to tell me the boys were coming and they were going to stay with us.

Because the city was so hot in the summer, Zach, Lennox and her boys all traveled to Wisconsin on the weekends to stay at our parents' summer home. On Saturday mornings, Zach and Lennox woke up late and left Russ and me in charge of her sons. In the afternoon, the couple excused themselves to go shopping in the surrounding areas. Lennox had a purpose for their shopping outing, she wanted to meet a portrait artist in order to commission a portrait of herself for her castle.

"We will be late returning today. So, can you watch the boys? I understand Gail and Russ are leaving early." Lennox inquired of Ruth.

"Oh course, Lennox, what will you and Zach be doing? What time do you think you will be home? Should I feed the kids?" Mother wanted to understand her new position as grandmother. She did not want to overstep herself.

"We will be back around seven. I found a portrait artist and I'm having a painting done of myself," Lennox confided in Mother. "It is so interesting. I have been going through books and books of royal paintings. The artist told me to choose a setting and he would paint my likeness. I don't have to sit for hours like my father the Duke and his relatives had to do." She said this in a rush. "But I still have to go for a few hours every weekend so the artist, Jack, can get a feel for my essence."

Mother looked at her with her eyebrows raised trying not to get mad. "Oh, what does Zach do?"

"Sometimes he comes in and reads but most of the time he just drops me off and goes somewhere. Why?" Lennox threw the "Why?" out with the tone of someone who suspects a fight is looming.

"No reason," Mother backed off. "OK, see you later."

As the summer drew to a close, Lennox invited Russ and me, Aunt Bev and Uncle Irv, and our parents to their Chicago apartment for the unveiling of the painting. Only Mother had seen their apartment—the rest of us had only heard from her about how fabulous it was.

We took the elevator up at the appointed hour.

"Just look for the Roman Ionic column in front of their door," Mother told us. "I just love this wallpaper and mirror the Lady chose for the hall. I think it gives it such class." She checked herself out in the mirror and reapplied her lipstick.

When Zach opened the door, we all took a collective breath. No one was prepared to see a massive crystal chandelier hanging in the six by six foyer. As we entered, Zach took everyone's coats and told us to please remove our shoes.

"Lennox purchased these Japanese slippers for each of you. I hope you like them." As our group bent down to remove our shoes, we noticed the foyer floor was tiled in a gray Italian marble.

"This is so overdone," Russ whispered to me. Their apartment was twelve hundred square feet and every square foot was filled. The massive furniture and ornate drapes were really meant for a space ten times larger.

Mother of course did not register this—she just saw the design touches that to her spoke of wealth and good taste.

Mother was very vocal as she escorted Irv and Bev through the apartment while Russ and I followed. "Doesn't Lennox have an eye for decorating, Bev? Can you believe how comfortable this carpet is? Did you see Zach's library? Did you see their magnificent bedroom set? Look at the bathroom." Mother went on exclaiming, her face flushed with pride.

Bev and Irv were a good audience. They gave the correct responses with nods and smiles. I wondered what they said when they left.

The first stop was the master bedroom, which had a theatrical Deco look. The massive bed was flanked by side tables which in turn supported two huge crystal lamps. Russ tapped my arm and signaled for me to raise my head. My jaw dropped—the entire ceiling was mirrored.

The second bedroom was Zach's library. It had three walls full of books. His antique desk was surrounded by his musical instruments: four guitars, a sitar, a cello, a mandolin, and a few other string instruments that I did not recognize.

The bathrooms had been remodeled with all new fixtures and terrazzo floors, and when we went into the small opening that leads to the studio apartment, we saw that the kitchen had been turned into a laundry room. Zach tried to move the group along, but that's when Russ pointed out the tanning bed in the center of the room. "Well," he whispered, "now we know where that tan comes from."

With the tour over, we were escorted back to the living room and asked to take our seats for dinner.

"Oh, your table is so beautiful, it should be in a home fashion magazine," gushed Mother.

Lennox's table was set with heavy silver candlesticks with white candles dripping the appropriate amount of wax. The table linens draped perfectly. The dishes, silverware, and napkins all displayed their royal crest. The crystal light fixture twinkled like stars on a clear spring night, giving the table setting a fairytale quality. Then there was a butler and a maid hired to serve the dinner.

Aunt Bev was enjoying her meal when something occurred to her. "You know it's funny. The other night Irv and I had dinner down the street. I remember having something that tasted like this there. Do you know the place? Have you ever been?" she asked innocently.

"No," was the Lady's curt reply

"Oh, I was just curious. It seems so similar." my aunt trailed off as she busied herself with her knife and fork.

Mother looked at her sister-in-law with displeasure. How could she question the Lady?

Russ, who had an eye for detail, had pointed out to me the foil pans in the kitchen before we were seated. After dessert it was time for the unveiling.

The Lady spoke, "As you know, Zach and I are going to be moving into our new castle in the fall. I wanted to have a portrait of myself completed for our new home. In England, the nobility have their portraits done and their descendants keep the paintings in their castles to show the world their lineage. Tell me what you think of this one." She pulled on the gold cord and the heavy emerald green velvet covering fell to the floor. The family all stared at the likeness on canvas.

"Oh, how beautiful," Mother exclaimed placing her hands on her face as though she was in shock.

Then we applauded, because we didn't know what else to do. When we left, we told the couple what a lovely evening we had. We kissed and uttered the appropriate formalities.

"Thank you, your portrait is wonderful, the apartment is gorgeous, and dinner was delicious."

The next day, I heard my mother talking to her friend. "Yes, Ester, David told me he thinks something is amiss because Lennox did not pay for the portrait. Yes, he told me the artist had called him at work today asking for payment of ten thousand dollars. When David asked him why the Lady did not pay him directly, the artist told David that the Lady said her father-in-law had commissioned the work. When David called Lennox, she told him she would consider it the perfect gift to give her in exchange for the cost of the trip. I guess it makes sense.

Chapter Sixteen
TROUBLE AND ACCUSATIONS

What my eyes can't see, my heart can't feel.

— HISPANIC PROVERB

In September, Lennox resumed her globetrotting ways. She was flying off to Scotland and staying for prolonged periods of time. When I asked her about her responsibilities at the brokerage firm, she looked at me with true disdain and said, "My boss granted me a leave of absence. He said I could come back whenever I want to. He is such a dear, I can never disappoint him. I am going to work for him when I return—that is if I have time. Right now, I am busy remodeling Tyninghame Castle."

This new story did not make any sense to me, "Mother, if Lennox is now wealthy and noble, why does she need to work as an executive assistant? It seems to me she should have quit her job by now."

"Gail, will you give it a rest. Lennox is capable of doing many things at once. She is even able to manage her boss's affairs from afar." She explained this to me as she instructed me on which clothes, she no longer wanted while I while I cleaned her closet.

For all his education, Zach had never learned how to manage his finances, because he really didn't need to. Zach never bothered to look at prices when he went shopping, nor did he ever look at the bank's statement that came at the end of the month. Zach gave this responsibility to Lennox, trusting her to take care of their investments. Therefore, he never questioned Lennox, even after the loan shark encounter. He figured his wife had learned her lesson, and after she came into her new wealth, he assumed all of their financial problems had been solved. Besides, Zach found these transactions distasteful and beneath him.

When Lennox called from Scotland asking him to forward their mail, Zach was surprised by the volume of bills they had received. But he did not question her. He simply put them in a large box as she had instructed and shipped them to her Scotland address.

On Valentine's Day 1988, I was happy and looking forward to the evening. Because it also was our son Nick's birthday, our family was going out to dinner to celebrate. Lennox had returned the day before from Scotland, so the entire family was going to be together.

That festive feeling dissipated rapidly around noon.

My husband and I worked for my father at the Dale Uniform Company. Russ managed the Fire Department Commissary. I paid the bills for the company and watched over my father.

I was working in my office when I was asked to take a call from Lennox's boss around one o'clock.

"Hello, Mr. Nero, can I help you with something?"

"Yes, I was looking for Dr. Dale, but cannot find him, so I thought to try his father. Is Mr. Dale there? I would like to speak with him."

"No, my father has just stepped out, but I can give you Zach's office number. I can also have my father call you when he returns."

Something felt off. I could not wait for Dad to return to the store. When I heard his voice, I rushed to give him the message from Lennox's boss, and as always, I dialed for him. When Mr. Nero started the conversation, Dad sat up straighter in his chair, and he seemed to have a hard time breathing. He looked as though he was going to faint.

"Dad, are you OK?"

"Gail, would you please leave the room and close the door."

This was really strange. He usually wanted me nearby and had never asked me to leave before. When he rang off, he got up and left the store. He did not even tell me he was leaving. I had no idea what was happening and I was worried. I called Mother but she did not pick up. Finally, she called to tell me they were not going to be able to celebrate Nick's birthday with us.

"Gail, Dad told me what happened today. Mr. Nero called to ask Dad if he knew where Lennox was. He wants to ask her about some questionable transactions. The accountants auditing the entertainment account found large amounts of money paid to vendors they did not recognize doing business with the firm. They needed to speak to Lennox, his executive assistant, about the vendors and transactions. It appears that many checks had been sent to her directly."

Mother was speaking hurriedly. "I really do not understand why he called Dad. When Dad called Zach, he learned Zach already knew that Mr. Nero was looking for them.

"Zach told me his friend Dr. Loew called him. Did you ever meet him, Gail? He is a psychiatrist who used to share space in Zach's downtown office. Dr. Loew told Zach that Lennox was with him and she had threatened to kill herself. Can you believe this story, Gail? I am so upset for Zach." Yes, I could hear the anxiety in her voice.

"Then what happened?" I asked. This just seemed to be yet another chapter in the life of Lady Bristol. "How did Lennox explain herself?" Because I was sure Lennox would pull an explanation out of the air. She could find a logical explanation for whatever appeared illogical.

"Oh, the poor girl was almost in a catatonic state, according to Zach. She appeared to hardly know him. She was crying and acting confused. Zach tried to comfort her, and promised to stay by her side forever. He is amazing, don't you think?"

I felt like I was listening to a soap opera and this series was called "The Days of Lady Bristol."

Mother continued, "Lennox said she needed to use the ladies' room. After fifteen minutes, when Lennox did not reappear, Zach went into the ladies' room but there was no sign of her."

"He went back to their apartment and found a note from her on the dining room table. Lennox told him it was all a big mistake and there was a logical explanation. She could fix it, she just needed time. She was going to Scotland and she would contact him from there. Zach is frantic. I wonder if Lennox really did the things Mr. Nero said. I wonder what is going to happen to Zach. I am so nervous."

Dad was nervous too—he knew who was going to end up paying the bill. And after how hard they both tried to make Zach's life perfect they both realized this scandal could be a huge detriment to Zach's reputation.

Suddenly, everything Russ had talked about made sense. When Russ came home from work, I told him what I learned.

"Gail, do you recall me showing you the section I read in the *Wall Street Journal* on how anyone could obtain a British title? All you had to do was buy a piece of land that carried a title from an existing British Lord's property. The Lord had the ability to grant these titles for a fee. This was the way the noble class was trying to support itself without funds from the British government. And now that you tell me she is an embezzler, it all falls into place. We could explain this to your parents tonight. But I doubt they will believe us."

He was probably right about that.

Chapter Seventeen
THANKSGIVING: VACATION DEMAND

> You have power over your mind – not outside events. Realize this, and you will find strength.
>
> — MARCUS AURELIUS

Lennox, now only to be referred to as Lady Bristol, had returned to Scotland. At the beginning of November, Zach called our mother, "Mom, I just spoke to Lennox. She is coming back to Chicago at the end of the month. She told me she would be here around Thanksgiving."

"That is good news Zach. Will she come for Thanksgiving dinner?"

"Of course. We will both come. Thanksgiving is my favorite holiday you know. I have some other news from her. We are going to go to Mexico in December for Christmas. She told me her father, the Duke, has a friend who owns a villa in Puerto Vallarta and they would not be using it. They offered it to the Duke, but he had other plans. So, he asked to let his daughter, Lady Bristol, use it. He has agreed! It's a large villa with more than five bedrooms, complete with a cook, driver, and housekeeper. Peter and the boys will be coming. We also invited her sister, Karson, and her husband from Canada, Zach informed his mother as if nothing has changed.

"I am so happy, you need a vacation," Mother replied. "You have been working lots of hours and I know that you miss her. It must really be hard to only communicate by phone. I am so glad she is coming back to Chicago. It has been a long time since we have seen Lennox. I think maybe almost nine months? I know you have been lonely. I will tell Gail the good news and to expect the two of you at her house for Thanksgiving."

Thanksgiving was always cold and many times welcomed the first snow of the year. Our large suburban house was a landmark prairie style home and somewhat drafty. The hot water steam system only took the chill out of the air for periods of time and when it got cold it took awhile for the system to react. Fall in Chicago was gray and cloudy, only accented by the colorful falling leaves. The color palate of my families clothing represented this season, usually dark gray or black. The uncles wore pullover sweaters under their jackets and the aunts dressed in long skirts with sweaters. The cousins dressed in slacks or blue jeans and turtlenecks.

Before Lady Bristol and Zach arrived, the only conversation was about them, in fact, they were always the only topic of conversation. How did Zach fit into this Cinderella story? What is happening between her and the brokerage firm? She had been gone so long. Was her new status going to affect their relationship? Was Zach really titled and was he moving to Scotland? Was their love strong enough to span this difference in social status? Was Zach willing to give up his practice, family, friends, and home in Chicago to move to Scotland with no vocation? Everyone heard about the charges from her former employer, but we had no details. We were all anxious to find out what she had done and why. Was it really a misunderstanding as Lennox had led us to believe? Everyone was walking on pins and needles, afraid to ask about her potential legal problems.

"What do you think Lennox will do when she gets here? Do you think she will tell us what happened?" asked the nosiest cousin, Diane.

"Yes, I wonder if we will learn the truth. Do you think it will affect her standing with her father, the Duke?" chuckled the social climbing cousin, Ida.

"I just wonder how we are all supposed to behave towards her now that we know she is a potential felon," I said as I finished organizing the table and the cousins looked at me in horror.

"How can you say such things, Gail? You must know there has to be a reasonable explanation." My mother corrected me as she entered into the kitchen. She had only entered the room to tell all her nieces they did not know how to make mashed potatoes.

We were accustomed to the royal couple being tardy so we started the ritual of enjoying our holiday feast. My parents sat at the head of the table joined by his brother and wife on the right. My mother's sister and husband sat next to her and the cousins filled in according to age. The children were delegated to a table of their own in the hall. Just as we were all seated and ready to dig into the buffet of holiday food, Zach and Lennox arrived, an hour and a half late. It felt as though a strong wind had blown them into the house, they came in laughing and as always, they brought expensive gifts for my aunts, uncles, and my children. I felt she was dressed even more outrageously on this evening. Her ensemble tonight was a long green skirt with a tight form fitting plaid jacket. Her overly tanned face accentuated her huge plaid hat that was pinned to her excessive amount of hair extensions, which was topped off with a peacock feather on the side. Her shoes were expensive. I could see they were made of velvet, vintage with a large crystal broach on each toe. I wondered how she could wear shoes like this in cold weather. Zach was wearing a brown plaid English sports jacket. He had grown a heavy mustache and he was smoking his pipe.

The couple appeared to be madly in love, touching each other and playing flirtatious word games, and laughing at their inside jokes. It was an interesting show, their appearance of being madly in love, making the family envious of their great connection and wishing they were more in the know. We all felt like outsiders when they were in our presence. On this night, my family was curious to see how they would behave towards each other since she was accused of a white-collar crime.

When they entered the house my family looked at them and a silence filled the room. I looked at my family and saw the same expression on their faces. "Do we all get up and hug her and say we are so sorry? Do we wait for her to cry and confess and tell her story? Or will my mother or father ask her directly what is going on?" But no, none of the above occurred.

My mother got up from her seat to hug her son and daughter-in-law. "Oh, Lady Bristol how beautiful you look. Gail, you and Russ need to get up and let Zach and the Lady sit down. Can you help them with their plates?" My husband Russ and I got up and obediently gave our seats in the dining room to them, prepared their plates, then we went to sit at the children's table located in the large front hall of our home.

When everyone sat down again to eat it was as though nothing had changed. The Lady and Zach monopolized the conversation, talking about their marvelous day and the plans they had for the upcoming Christmas holiday. Zach's opening statement set the tone for the Thanksgiving dinner.

"Lady Bristol was offered a villa in Puerto Vallarta, complete with servants for the Christmas and New Year's holidays." Zach told everyone at the dining room table. "Her father, the Duke, has a wealthy friend who owns it. The villa has nine rooms. There are five bedrooms, a pool, and three servants who work there full time. Because of the problems she has been having, the Duke offered his villa to her." Zach and the Lady looked toward me and continued, "So we were wondering if you and your family would like to come?"

I looked at Zach in total disbelief and confusion. This was the only mention of "her potential problem" all night. I could not believe everyone was still falling for her stories. But, not only did Zach believe this to be true, so did my parents! My mother was beaming, she was so happy for me. She said she wanted me to have the wonderful experience similar to the one she had with the Lady in Europe. My mother felt I was so lucky to have been included. I felt as though this was a set up. I believed that this was discussed beforehand and now after all the plans were organized, I was informed in front of the entire family. What ingratitude I would show if I did not agree to this trip and thank them profusely for the invitation.

"The villa is in Puerto Vallarta. I think you will enjoy it. You like to speak Spanish," was my mother's final word.

Later, over the course of the dinner, I learned Zach and Lady Bristol were originally slated to go with her family. But her father was not feeling well. They had asked her sister in London to join them, but her children were busy. Her sister in Toronto was going to spend the holiday with her husband's family. I guess by process of elimination they had room available for my family. I looked at my red-headed mother who was nodding her head so vigorously that she was starting to look like a bobble head doll. I smiled at her and thought, "I don't want to do this." I could not see Russ to ask what he wanted to do, I felt my family staring at me and wondering what was taking me so long to say "OK." And when I did, my family cheered, because that is what we do.

Chapter Eighteen
PUERTO VALLARTA HOLIDAY

By failing to prepare, you are preparing to fail.

— BENJAMIN FRANKLIN

I arrived at the Puerto Vallarta International Airport on December eighth with my daughter, Tracy, and son, Nick. My husband, Russ, did not accompany us. My father said Russ had to stay and work at the Dale Uniform Company store to help close out the year. He would be coming at the end of the second week. I was going to spend the bulk of the Christmas holidays with my children, Zach, my sister-in-law, and her three boys, without the support of my husband. I was nervous as I disembarked the plane, walked down the stairs, and boarded a crowded bus to get to the terminal holding my small children's hot little hands. It was sunny and warm, unlike the Chicago winter day I had just left a couple of hours before. I was led to Mexican customs where I had to produce identification and birth certificates for my children and myself. This was the time before passports were needed to visit Mexico. I pressed the button that determined if I had to do additional screening. Luckily it came up green. I paid the entrance fees and gathered the necessary tourist forms.

Exiting customs, I found Zach waiting for us outside the arrival area at the airport. He was alone and almost dancing with excitement. This was a characteristic Zach had never displayed before, nothing ever seemed to faze him.

"Gail, wait until you see the villa." He was driving a black Volkswagen sedan, very upscale and regal. I put our luggage away and climbed in. He told us that we were going to a special place high up on a mountain in this quaint Mexican village. We piled into the car and he drove very fast through the narrow winding streets with lots of speed bumps. It was very disturbing to look out at the poverty of the homes and stores of this tourist village.

"The villa looks like something from the movie Robinson Crusoe." He told me, with a huge smile on his face as he was leaning towards the steering wheel trying to navigate the bumpy road. "The house is high up on a mountain and the most amazing thing about the house is that the windows do not have any glass. They are totally open, the city and ocean views are unbelievable. The villa totally blends into the mountain because it is built with natural local materials. Lennox and I are on the second floor and our room is the length and width of the villa. You will have the room off the living room and your kids will be downstairs with the boys. We are almost there, Gail. Wait until you see the house."

I sat in the car and looked out the window and wondered why I had decided to join Zach and Lennox. Looking at the back seat where my children sat, I asked myself how we were going to survive this trip. I knew Lennox did not like them and I was never sure of Zach's commitment to me. The trip from the airport to the house took about forty-five minutes.

"Zach, everything is so dusty and dirty. I haven't seen a clean paved street, just shabby houses that look like they are about to fall in on themselves. And is that a dead horse on the road? Was that some sort of roadside memorial?" I asked as I gazed out the window.

At last, Zach turned off the highway onto a random road that had no signage and headed up a narrow unpaved gravel path. As we wound up the steep hill full of abandoned half-finished buildings overrun with vegetation, Zach became more excited and started drumming the steering wheel. "Yes, these are local homes, and yes they are built of salvaged materials and this is an unpaved street. Really Gail, get with it." Zach gave me a look that I was very familiar with, "And as we get closer to the top of the mountain, you will see a small hotel where the road becomes paved with curbs." The look was contempt. He didn't think I would fit in and now I was proving it by my dumb comments. Passing the hotel, Zach turned to the left and said, "We are almost there. Wait until you see the house."

The car passed a large 25-foot shear stone wall and then turned the corner. There was a beautifully painted sign in green and pink proclaiming the name of the villa: La Casa de Las Brisa's. Zach parked the car on a huge circular driveway. The house did indeed resemble a tree house, being on top of the mountain. It was a two-story tan stucco house with a pitched thatched roof made up of banana leaves. When I walked up the stone walkway into the house, I was in awe, it was beautiful. It was as though I had stepped into a movie set. When I entered the house and looked up, I saw the staircase leading up to the room Zach and Lennox were sharing. It looked like a tree house from the inside as well. The second floor was supported by a large tree-like column and the winding carved bamboo staircase looked and smelled as though it were built by a Native American Indian Tribe from Oklahoma. Everywhere I looked I saw rainforest type materials held together by products resembling corn husks. The villa looked sturdy and exciting.

The deep blue kitchen was off to the right and there were three women preparing food. In the center was the dining area, painted a hue of bright pink, it overlooked the pool down below. There were no walls, just one huge open space. Because there was no glass in the windows, we were more exposed to the outdoors, meaning bugs and sounds. The interior of the house was full of color tones that screamed Mexico. There were bright woven Mexican blankets and pillows placed on all the couches and chairs. All the bedrooms had beautiful woven bedspreads and mosquito netting.

My bedroom was to the left of the entry. I was told my room had a view towards the town and the ocean, but I could not see anything through the trees. There were three bedrooms on the lower level where my children and Lennox's three boys would be sleeping. The rooms were like caves because they were sunk underneath the house and built of stone. Each of the rooms faced the elliptical swimming pool, deck, and large garden. This did not seem to be the right place for the children to sleep, it seemed dangerous with the pool so near. Lennox assured me that it was ok, the pool was lit and it was a long distance from the rooms.

Once my family was settled, I thought everyone would be having dinner together since I saw the three ladies cooking in the kitchen. Then I learned about the gay couple Lennox and Zach had met living next door. This couple had adopted a young boy around ten years old.

"Gail, you must be so tired from your trip." Lennox spoke to me! This was the first time she spoke to me since she became Lady Bristol. She usually had Zach tell me her bidding. "I made plans for Zach and me to go out with our neighbors tonight. I invited their son to come over. He is a darling boy and he is alone. I had the maids prepare dinner for all of you. We will be leaving soon. See you tomorrow." And off they went. Now my role was clear. I was to be the nanny for this trip.

The next morning, I dressed and went downstairs to get the children ready for the day. When we came up, Zach and the boys were sitting around the large, round dining room table waiting to be served breakfast from the staff.

"Good morning everyone. Am I late for breakfast?" I asked "I see everyone is eating, has Lennox already finished?"

"No, she hasn't come down yet. It takes Mom a while to get dressed." Her oldest answered.

Just as Zach and I were finishing our morning coffee, Lennox appeared. She was wearing a tight fitting, long, black beach gown, with a heavy beaded sparkling necklace. On her ears were huge diamonds, and on her wrist were many bracelets of all different colors that contextualized with the walls of the house. Her hair was pulled back and she had it covered with a tight-fitting scarf. I suddenly realized she must have had her extensions removed for this trip.

I became upset, because before I left, I had asked Lennox what type of clothes I should pack. "Oh, you won't need much." Lennox told me in an off handed way, "We are staying at the villa. We will be eating there too. During the day we will go to the beach. So just bring comfortable clothes and one or two bathing suits."

So that is what I did. I packed comfortable clothes for myself and the kids. But now I realized Lennox had again made me look the fool.

Everyone learned to wait for Lennox each morning. She appeared each morning in incredible outfits, complete with accessories. Once she had her coffee she told us what our plans were for the day. We had to go in two cars: Zach drove one with Lennox, and one of the staff drove me with all the children. When we arrived and settled ourselves at the beach, Zach and the Lady disappeared. I was left with the responsibility of all the children.

I could not understand what possessed me to agree to this trip. Oh, yes, I do. My mother made me do it. Perhaps my mother thought, on this trip, alone with Lennox, she would talk and I would learn what happened in Chicago. But no, the fantasy lived on. Every day we drove to different beaches, and once settled, Lennox and Zach disappeared only to reappear when it was time to return to the villa. As soon as we returned to the villa everyone went to their respective rooms to regroup. Zach took his preferred chair in the living room reading, perhaps he understood it was Lennox's time to be alone in her second-floor retreat. I was never invited upstairs to see it so I had no idea what that area was like. Once everyone showered and dressed, we sat by the pool. But Lennox never joined us because she would be waiting for different service people each day.

The doorbell would ring, the staff answered the door and showed them up towards the circular staircase to see the Lady. There were people from the area salons that she had contacted to come to the house to give her facials and body massages and women to do her nails, wax her legs, fix her hair, and just to pamper her. She never went to the shops, the shops came to her. I would sit by the pool and watch the five children and the neighbor's son play and eat nachos that the kitchen staff had prepared. Zach would be reading in the shade. Then promptly at six, dinner was served for the children and me. The royal couple would leave to go out with the gay couple next door.

Two weeks later, Russ finally joined the group. I was never so happy to see him, my heart was pumping so hard. I really needed his support, and his perspective. Before I left the house with the driver to pick Russ up at the airport, Lennox gave me a command.

"Be sure you rent a car at the airport. My driver will not be at your service anymore. I have business to do and I will be needing him."

We rented a yellow beetle convertible, my dream car. But it only caused Lennox to explode. "Why would you rent a selfish car like a Volkswagen beetle? Didn't you know you have to drive my children too? Besides, that car looks terribly tacky in front of the villa. Tomorrow I want you to exchange it. Also, why did you buy Frosted Flakes and donuts? You know my boys will not eat that kind of food. What were you thinking?" She only told us to rent a car, she hadn't given any specifics. We had assumed it was for our family as she had one for hers. Russ said he would not return the car, he liked the open air of the beetle and so did I. And the next morning her boys were fighting over the *Zucaritos*, Spanish for Frosted Flakes.

One of the daily trips recommended by the gay neighbors involved driving south of town to a small fishing village. In order to get to *La Playa de Las Animas*, Lennox hired a small fishing boat with a dinghy. Once we reach the isolated beach shore, we all had to climb into this small craft, thank goodness the waves were calm. The only activity on the wide white sand beach were several pop up restaurants. It was lacking the tourist crowds perhaps because it was a gay beach. Lennox and Zach immediately went to the restaurant area leaving Russ and me on the beach with six children who started to question us about what they observed.

"Mom, why are those men kissing?" our son asked.

"Nick, those men are in love, please look away and give them some privacy."

Finally, the three weeks were over and our family went home. I had never wanted to leave a place so much. I could not believe that after staying in a house for three weeks with Lennox I was no closer to her than I was when we had first met eight years ago. Russ and I only had one night out with the royal couple. On this night, Lennox told us how Zach was going to leave his practice and move with her to Scotland. Life just went on for her, she did not seem in the least bit stressed.

They both kept on shopping and living the life you would imagine royalty led. The royal couple remained in Mexico for three more weeks.

"Good morning Gail, Dad and I are going out to dinner tonight with Zach and Lady Bristol. We are going to a new Mexican restaurant where the Lady made reservations. I don't like Mexican food, but I am sure we will have a wonderful evening. Lennox told us since they were in Mexico, they discovered the cuisine to be wonderful. She wants to share her new-found taste treats with us. Isn't she darling" To this day I still wonder why my mother felt compelled to tell me about their dinner dates with the Lady and Zach. Russ and I were never included in any of the extravagant evening meals.

The next day, I learned about the dinner, "Good morning Mom. How was your evening? Did you enjoy the restaurant?" I really was not interested in hearing about their experience, it was always the same—Zach was brilliant and Lennox was gorgeous. But I was curious if Lennox spoke of her crime to them. I was sure my mother would have pried or extracted some information out of them. However, now when Zach was asked anything, he got mad and walked away or his eyes would float away from you as though his body had floated away as well. He was never going to go against his ideal British wife, Lady Bristol.

"Dinner was wonderful. Your brother and Lennox looked so tan and rested. Your Dad and I enjoyed the restaurant. We even saw some friends of ours there. They enjoyed meeting your brother and the Lady. Zach has a way of making everyone he meets so comfortable. And Lennox has wonderful stories to tell. We stayed there quite late. It was fun."

"That's nice. Did you learn anything about what is going to happen to Lennox? Did she mention anything having to do with the charges? Will she need to get a lawyer to defend herself? Was it really a misunderstanding and she was able to explain everything?"

"What kind of girl did I raise? No, we did not talk about it. I bet the whole thing blows over. I am sure it was all a mistake. Oh, yes, Lennox told us that you left a lot of money there for her. Don't you understand pesos? You really should be more careful with how you spend your money."

I thought this was a weird statement coming from my mother who subsidized her son. All I could do was roll my eyes and take a deep breath so that I would not say anything to upset her. But I thought "Why doesn't my mother remember that I am the one who is able to live on a budget?" I was afraid of my parents. They were generous, but on their terms. Zach, on the other hand was not afraid to let them know he needed funds and how much.

I kept wondering how Lennox escaped the law. Everything appeared to be working out for her. Her stories were so farfetched. People on the street were still giving her jewelry, and now designers were giving her clothes to wear.

"Yes, it's crazy isn't it? The young designers are calling me and asking me to wear their clothes. Lucien is the hottest designer in Chicago now and he told me I was better advertising than magazines."

According to Lennox, the designers felt she could sell their designs because women wanted to look like her. I felt she looked plastic, like a Barbie Doll.

Chapter Nineteen
THE LADY'S LAST APPEARANCE

I came, I saw, I conquered.

— JULIUS CAESAR

Our daughter, Tracy, was turning thirteen and becoming a bat mitzvah. All our relatives and Tracy's friends were invited to the temple to see her perform the service. I was not sure if my brother and Lady Bristol were coming, especially given the questions swirling around her. When I made my eight-thirty phone call on the morning of the celebration, Mother told me, "Yes, they are coming! It's wonderful we will all be together. However, Zach and the Lady will be leaving early because she must fly back to Scotland tonight. Zach is going to join her next week. He told me he will be staying in Scotland for two weeks organizing their new castle." Mother was so excited for him because she felt he really needed a rest.

As we were buzzing around getting ready for the service, Zach and Lennox surprised us by arriving early. I was fully expecting Mother to make the service wait for them. It was a relief to be able to focus on my child on her big day.

Tracy did marvelously. I was very impressed and relieved. My father had been talking throughout the service about the content. The rabbi's sermon was on the use of the word "He" not "She" in the Bible. My father found this quite disturbing and he was starting to act out. I became anxious never knowing where his *mishegas* (crazy behavior) would start or end.

With the service concluded, we held her celebration in a room at the temple. I stood in the corner with my friends looking out at the dance floor, it was a warm day for June and I noticed that everyone was dressed in casual, comfortable outfits. Looking at Lennox prancing her way up to people, I had to wonder as I turned towards my cousin. "Don't you think she's dressed a little over the top?"

"No, you don't understand fashion," replied Ida, the social climber from California. "This is what the stars are wearing now."

"We haven't seen her in a long time," another cousin murmured to me. "Your mom was telling us about the amazing trip to Scotland she took them on. But she didn't mention anything about the legal issues. Did someone say something about misappropriations of funds?" This line of inquiry made me uncomfortable, to say the least.

Thankfully, one of my girlfriends jumped in with her opinion. "She does draw a crowd. Look at the way the men are all flocking to her. She is giving each one a royal minute." My friends and I were standing in a huddle observing the Lady, and I thought we must look like what Shakespeare called "obdurate shrews." But I was nonetheless glad to be among friends.

Lady Bristol had not been seen in over six months and once again she came dressed like she was attending the Oscars instead of a simple family celebration. On Tracy's day to shine, Lennox was the center of attention, dressed rather too flamboyantly (in my opinion) for the occasion. Her makeup was flawless and she must have had some more plastic surgery because there was not a wrinkle on her skin. All eyes were on her and she knew it.

The Lady was in rare form, laughing and chatting with all my friends. Previously, I felt she thought my friends were beneath her status because in the past she'd just nod her head to recognize their presence, but this time she was engaged in the activities. Yet something just did not seem right.

Lady Bristol delighted and really surprised the guests when she took part in the hula-hoop contest. Everyone watched her because the sight of the dignified Lady with a hula-hoop circling her twenty-inch slim waist was a strange sight. I wondered if her fake hair was going to get caught or if her short skirt would expose something *un*ladylike.

Everyone at the party was speculating about her. We all knew she had done something illegal while working at the brokerage firm. I wondered why she came to the party, because she had fled the country under suspicious circumstances. But nobody had the nerve to ask her about the situation with her former employer. We all treated her as though she was a celebrity, therefore no one dared to ask her about her personal life. And Lennox used our fear to her advantage, knowing our family never would offend Zach. So instead, we all watched her perform with wide-eyed wonder.

The memory of Tracy's bat mitzvah was overshadowed by the appearance and actions of Lady Bristol. Why was she in Chicago for this special family celebration? So many questions, but we wouldn't get any answers that day. With her charm and intellect, she controlled everyone and everything around her. The stories were hers to tell, and if pressed, she could change the subject.

When Lady Bristol left the celebration, it was the last time we would see her for ten years.

Chapter Twenty
THE DEPARTURE

That which does not kill us makes us stronger.

— FRIEDRICH NIETZSCHE

Still claiming her title required her presence in her fiefdom, the Lady was spending more and more time in Scotland. I believe even Zach was confused by the turn of events, yet he still maintained belief in his wife and was anxious to be with her again. After the bat mitzvah, Lennox left for her castle in Scotland and the plan was for Zach to join her in two weeks.

When Zach called our parents from Europe, everything in his life changed. My mother told me what happened because he needed my help.

"Gail, Zach called us from Venice."

"Why is he in Venice, Mom. I thought you told me he was going to fly to England to see his new castle."

"Well, his flight was to Heathrow Airport. Gail, let me tell you what happened, don't interrupt me. Oh vey, where was I, oh yes, before he left for the airport, Lennox called to remind him to check their mailbox and not to bother going through the mail. You know Zach, he never thinks about mail or bills. He told me he had only checked his mailbox once before, therefore he remembered to bring a box with him to collect two weeks' worth."

"*Kine-ahora* (don't give me the evil eye), he called me before he left, he was so excited to leave the city and he was anxious to see Lennox. You know how Zach gets when he is happy and full of excitement, his voice is so much fun to hear. Well, I understood his excitement with the prospect of seeing their new castle and the British nobility. What a snob he is. We really had the most marvelous time in England with the Lady." Mother said this with a little giggle as I rolled my eyes. "When he went to get the mail as Lennox reminded him to do, he couldn't get all the mail out because the small box was stuffed. On top of the pile of mail was a note informing him to check with Margo, the building manager, to get his additional mail. I can't believe Margo didn't call him. Your father really should replace her."

"When he returned to his apartment, he thought he should go through the mail to separate the junk from invitations to parties, he never thought there would be invoices. He told me he spotted a thick envelope that was from an insurance company and he opened it. He was shocked to find a policy insuring his life. If he died, Lennox was the sole beneficiary of five-million-dollar whole life plan! Among the many envelopes, he found statements from four credit card companies. There were three MasterCard statements, one for each of Lennox's children with his name as payee. He put the Visa, MasterCard, Diner's Club, and American Express invoices together and started to open them. Even after we paid off the moneylender, can you believe he still relied on Lennox to manage their financial affairs? You know Zach never balanced a checkbook in his life. He just wrote checks assuming there was money in the bank. Zach told me these bills amounted to over a couple hundred thousand dollars!"

"He was so upset, I can just picture my darling boy. Then he told me he called her and demanded to know how she could have spent this much money. He thought he was going to have a heart attack. You should have heard his voice, when he told me about this part of the story, his voice was so deflated. I felt such *tsoriss* (trouble)."

"He told me she asked why he opened the mail. And she assured him not to be nervous. She told him she did not want to waste time on the phone and that she would explain everything to him when they were together."

As Mother told me this story, I was imaging Lennox and how she instinctively knew how to calm and charm her prey. It was hard for me to feel sorry for Zach; in many ways I felt he had this hardship coming. I saw him as a lazy person, he, like our mother, relied on his looks. And Mother was always acting as his public relations representative, telling everyone how smart he was and touting his experience as a doctor. He had no hubris. He, like both of our parents, never dealt with confrontation. Therefore, it was easier for him to trust his wife and not fight. He wanted to believe in their charmed make-believe life.

Mother continued, "When he landed at Heathrow Airport the next day, Lennox was not there. Instead, after clearing customs, he saw a man carrying a sign with his name on it. He approached the man and identified himself. Zach, made a point of telling me the chauffeur's name because he felt it was so common, it was John. Then, Zach started imitating John, talking in his British accent reenacting how John spoke to him, 'The Lady sent me to retrieve you and your luggage and to escort you to the small airport nearby.' Your brother is so adorable. Well, he told me he was aggravated, disturbed, and worried about the insurance policy. Perhaps this man was sent to kill him. He does have a vivid imagination, your brother. But he felt John was honest, so he proceeded to the black luxury sedan. You know Zach, when he was telling me this part of the story, I could tell this type of extravagance did not faze him. He said it was a short drive to the private airstrip where he saw Lennox waiting. I had to ask how she was dressed. He told me she was dressed as an aviator, complete with a white scarf around her neck that was blowing in the wind. Lennox really has style."

"She told him they were flying to Venice. And she booked a Cessna Citation Jet to take them there. Remember, my girlfriend's husband flew this type of plane. Zach was puzzled, because he believed they were going to their new castle in Scotland. She told him on the phone that she had had it remodeled and she was anxious to show it to him.

But she changed their plans because she wanted to go with him to a romantic place where they could relax and enjoy themselves."

"He asked her again, "Why are we going to Venice? Telling her Scotland was fine and that he really wanted to talk to her quietly about the bills. She told him to calm down, explaining she booked this trip to the Hotel Cipriani, when she heard the stress in his voice and she felt it would be a better place to discuss their finances."

"When they landed at the Marco Polo Airport in Venice, the hotel's private jetty was waiting to take them to San Marco on the Island of Giudecca. Zach had never been to Italy and he told me he had to admit the Lady had found an enchanting, peaceful setting."

"Zach said Lennox appeared happy and she was more talkative on the trip. She booked a six-star hotel located on three acres on Giudecca Island. I remember how she liked to educate us on our trip and I guess nothing changes because she told him this hotel was built in 1858 by Giuseppe Cipriani, he is the inventor of Zach's favorite cocktail 'Bellini.' Can you believe Zach remembered this fact? He is so smart."

"Zach, said he was calming down as he looked at the turquoise water and marveled at the grand architecture of the palaces and churches along the waterway. He recognized Saint Mark's Square and The Doges Palace from the books he has read. As their private launch neared the hotel and docked between the famous black and white striped poles, three bellhops from the hotel came to help them disembark and took their luggage. He remembered how the hotel's attendants were dressed in bright blue jumpsuits and how they addressed them with the respect required of royalty. The bellman held a royal blue umbrella with the crest of their hotel over their heads to protect them from the sun. I can picture this. Zach, must have walked with pride. "Lennox booked The Palazzo Vendramin suite for them. I believe that's what it is called. I have the statement in front of me. Zach told me The Palazzo is a 15th century palace and it is linked to the hotel by a courtyard and a garden. And their suite had a breathtaking water view of Venice and their own small private garden. It reminded me of the accommodations Lennox organized for us on our trip. I *kvell* (feel happy or proud) when I think of that trip."

"When they entered their suite, Zach took out his briefcase of outstanding bills and the five-million-dollar insurance policy. And asked her to explain how they were going to pay these bills and most of all why did she have this insurance policy."

"Her quick response was, 'Most of the bills have already been paid off. And all of her personal accounts are being paid by her solicitor in Scotland.' She told him that she made arrangements for her solicitor to track down the invoices and change the billing addresses. The bills and statements should have gone to her employee. And she did not understand why they came to their Chicago address."

"Then he asked her, how can you explain this life insurance policy?"

"And the Lady looked at him and told him he sounded paranoid. And if he knew anything about estate planning, he would know that a life insurance policy is the cornerstone of any plan, and that there are other pieces including investments."

"This sounded plausible to him. He felt her explanation made sense. She assured him there would be no more bills when he returned to Chicago. I asked Dad if we had a life insurance policy plan and he assured me we did. Do you?"

I believe I rolled my eyes at this question. "OK, mom, so what happened? Why do you sound so upset? Why does Zach need my help?"

"Well, I am getting to it Gail. Give me a chance. The next day, Lennox suggested they go sightseeing, but at the last minute she begged off, saying she wanted to sit by the pool. Zach said he understood her desire to stay at the hotel, because Lennox had been to Venice before and the Cipriani was known for its magnificent Olympic-size heated pool. Lennox told him she booked a historic walking tour for him using the hotel's concierge. The tour left at nine and was over at two. They planned to be together again at three to have cocktails. As he boarded the launch to take the tour, he told me he kept feeling as though someone was watching him. The life insurance policy was making him paranoid and suspicious. You know, Zach has always had thoughts about his mortality. Anyway, he told me he never saw anyone following him, but felt a presence. While he was touring, he made sure he was standing inside the circle of other tourists. Never letting himself be isolated from the group. When he returned to the hotel, Lennox was not at the pool nor in their suite. He told me it seemed strange that she was not in either locations. Knowing her he decided she was at the salon. But when it became four o'clock and she didn't return, he went to the salon to look for her. Not finding her there he went down to the lobby to ask if there were any messages for him."

"And the receptionist's told him, "No, sir, however, your wife did leave the hotel with her luggage around two pm." He told Zach that he was on duty and ordered the transport."

"Zach told me he stood in front of the receptionist and felt like he was going to pass out, but knew he had to control his emotions in this elegant establishment. The desk clerk asked him, "Shall I prepare your bill to settle the account?"

"When the clerk presented the statement for the room, Zach was shocked to find that the total was seven thousand dollars a night! He did not have that much money in his bank account, but he did have two credit cards in his wallet, they were both declined. That's the story he told me when he called me this morning. Now I need you to go to the store. You will need to help your father wire money to Zach right away."

"Ok, Mom. How much does he need? And do you have the wire transfer information in order to expedite the funds?" I asked these questions as though I was an employee rather than a daughter who really cared. Mother did not hear me. She wanted to tell the rest of Zach's story:

"Zach had to call me collect this morning. He is so frustrated and confused. He was crying into the phone when he told me Lennox left him. He told me he had no money to return home nor to pay the hotel bill. He told me his credit cards were all declined and he had no way of purchasing a plane ticket to return." at this point her voice cracked and I could hear her losing control of her own emotions.

"I tried to calm him down and told him, 'Of course. Dad is at the store. I will call him and let him know you are stranded. How much money do you need?"

Dad and I made the arrangements to pay the hotel bill using a wire transfer from his bank. With the help of the hotel and Dad's credit cards, Zach was able to purchase a plane ticket back to Chicago. The hotel put him up for an additional night in a less glamorous room. It took him two additional days in Venice and London to get back to Chicago.

When he opened the door to his apartment, he was in for another shock. He discovered all his furniture was gone. There was only the mattress to their bed lying on the bedroom floor. All his books, the bookcases, his desk, his instruments, and the pictures on the walls were gone, even the dining room chandelier. All the walls were bare. He could not believe it, he had absolutely nothing.

I learned this part of the story from Joseph, the building engineer. He told me Zach looked very pale as he confronted him to ask if he knew that he was robbed.

"No, Dr. Dale, you were not robbed." Joseph told him "the Lady told me to prepare your apartment and the other apartments for the moving company that did the pickup last week."

"'What other apartments?" Zach asked. Joseph told me he was surprised that Zach was not aware of how Lennox stored their belongings.

"Well, I thought you knew. Whenever an apartment was vacant, the Lady filled it with the furniture she bought. She told me she was sending the furniture to your castle in Scotland."

"How many apartments did she use?"

"At first two, she used the apartments to store her clothes, then when her boys and father came, she used two more. But when she started to buy the furniture, I guess we were up to five. The truck that came to pick up your things had to come back three times. Is everything OK? I hope I have not done anything wrong?"

Zach could not believe what he was hearing. Now he was sure he was being followed in Italy. Perhaps he was even being followed now.

Mother wanted to see for herself what happened to his apartment. Therefore, on my eight-thirty call Mother asked me, "Gail, would you pick me up and take me to Zach's apartment today? I want to see for myself if she really cleaned him out."

We arrived to find the apartment empty, except for ten fur coats, which had just arrived from storage that morning. And of course, Lennox did not take her tanning bed because the electrical service is different in Europe.

"The apartment looks like one of your tenants moved out in a hurry." Mother reported to Dad, "You can see the outlines of where furniture had rested on the heavy layered carpet. The tile floors are dirty with dust and bits of paper. And I can see where the artwork was hung on the walls. Gail is going to take me shopping. I want to purchase a bed, dishes, pots, pans, towels, and linens to help Zach cope with his loss. I am also going to ask one of the engineers if they could clean up the apartment, maybe even paint."

Mother went through the apartment like she was hunting for treasure. She found two beautiful hair combs and gave them to me.

"Here Gail, take these. I know they are worth a lot of money." she folded them into my hands as though she were as though she were giving me a wonderful gift.

She looked over the furs and took two, one to keep for herself and one to give to her sister. The others she left behind. She never offered me a fur and I never had the courage to ask.

Every day, debt collectors from the credit card companies were calling Zach. He was being hunted down. They called him in the middle of the night, at work, even at our parents' home. He could no longer obtain a credit card because of the unpaid debts. His bank account had been drained, and Dad had it closed. Our parents once again paid all his bills.

Upon reflection I believe the reason why Lennox came to our daughter's bat mitzvah was to make the arrangements with the building engineer and the moving company to ship their furniture and her clothing to Scotland.

Sara Lee reported this part of the story to me:

About ten days later, Lennox called Zach from Canada. She told him she was staying in a lovely rental apartment in a fashionable hotel in Toronto, but she would not tell him which one. She did not even begin her conversation with him by saying hello.

She told him, "I think it best if we divorce. I am here in Toronto with my boys. I realize now I should never have left them. I am going to stay here and make a new life for myself. Oh, yes, by the way, I realized when I left, I did not take my furs. I had them shipped from storage. I understand they arrived after the movers left. Please send them to me."

Sara Lee told me Zach didn't know how to respond. She reported that Zach wanted her back. I couldn't believe it. She had abandoned him in Venice, took all his belongings, he was now penniless, plus he felt she hired a hit man to kill him, yet he was still in love with her? Sara Lee told me he asked her why she wanted a divorce because he loved her and was going to stand by her.

And Lennox told Zach that she felt it is time they both moved on! She wanted this divorce. And she wanted him to tell our parents that she also wanted one hundred and fifty thousand dollars in cash not to implicate him, let's just say, "in their little scandal!" She told him she was going to call him at his parent's home that evening.

Zach asked her about his books, his tapes, and musical instruments. He wanted to know if she was going to return his medical textbooks and manuals. With that question in the air, the phone clicked. Zach was beside himself, and on reflex, called Mother.

"Mom, I just spoke to Lennox. She wants a divorce and one hundred and fifty thousand in cash, and her furs. She is going to call us at your apartment tonight at seven."

Zach took a cab and arrived at our parents' apartment around six in the evening. Lennox called at seven on the dot, Dad answered the phone as we all stood by and waited to hear the Lady's demands.

"Lennox, Zach just told us about your proposal. I feel as though you are blackmailing us." Dad spoke, trying to sound kind and understanding. Mother stood next to Zach to try to calm him. I was standing by the kitchen sink watching.

"Don't look at it that way, Dad. Look at it as Zach being released from his obligations and potential exposure to his reputation. You have taken care of him his whole life. What is a little more?"

Dad became very angry at her flippant remarks "What are you saying? Are you saying you plan on incriminating Zach?"

"Well, he did benefit and so did your family. I guess you could call this protection money. The price can go up if you wait too long. I will call you again next week."

Our parents decided to accept her demands and conditions, they did not want anything hanging over their nor Zach's heads. Life would continue and they paid her price.

When Lennox called the following week, Dad told her they would pay. Lennox laughed out loud when she heard the money was going to be wired to her Swiss bank account. They felt they could see her dancing.

Chapter Twenty-One
NOTHING EVER CHANGES

A journey of a thousand leagues begins beneath one's feet.

— LAO TZU

You would think this would have been the end of the story. Lennox *aka* Lady Bristol had taken everything from Zach: his credit, his prized musical instruments, vinyl records, book collection, medical textbooks and manuals, and his pride. You would think Lennox would have moved on and no one would ever hear from her again. But no, she kept in touch with Mother's sister, Sara Lee. On the one hand, Mother could not believe this betrayal from her own sister. After all, Zach was devastated and lucky to be alive. Nevertheless, Mother was happy that her sister was in contact with Lennox. She still loved Lennox and through her sister she learned about her life in Toronto. Lennox's divorce from Zach took six months. Through Sara Lee, we learned Lennox was getting married for the third time. We were not surprised because we had seen her work her charm on men so many times. Sara Lee told us she had found a wealthy Canadian businessman who wanted to marry her.

"He is crazy about me," Sara Lee recalled her saying. "He loves my boys, too. He is very rich, you know. We are buying a penthouse condo facing Lake Ontario in the most fashionable area in Toronto. It has a fabulous view, and there will be bedrooms for my boys when they stay with me."

"How did you meet him?" was Sara Lee's only question. She was happy for Lennox.

"I met him at a coffee house. I was reading the paper and he approached me. We went out a few times and then he asked me to marry him. It was very quick. You know his father owns a craft store franchise in Canada."

Lennox told Sara Lee her new husband had purchased a hair and body spa franchise for her and her oldest son Jordan. Their plan was to start with this one then open many throughout Toronto.

"Jordan is going to do the marketing, and I am going to run the operations. We found a good location downtown. It is so much fun working with my darling boy!"

This is how we also heard that her youngest son, Andy, was modeling for GQ magazine in England. What was not mentioned in her phone conversations was the story of her middle son, Henry. Mother knew Henry had dropped out of school at the age of sixteen to follow the Grateful Dead.

"Sara Lee, why don't you and Barney come to visit? Lennox asked. "You live so close and Barney does enjoy driving." But she really had an ulterior motive. Sara Lee was her link to Zach. She needed to know if anyone was looking for her.

When Sara Lee returned home from her visit, she called at her appointed time of eight: "Lennox looked beautiful. She married an older man named Fredrick. He is very refined. You should see her condo. It's enormous, with a panoramic view of the lake. She chose modern furniture. Everything was white! It was so different in style from the apartment and castle she shared with Zach. Her husband, Fredrick is a real gentleman. He treated us to dinner. Barney enjoyed him, too. We did not see the boys, but she did take us to see her salon. It was the most decadent experience. The spa was done up like a bordello in deep reds and purples. The staff all dressed in black tight dresses. You know Lennox, she has style."

About a year later, Sara Lee who was still in touch with Lennox, reported this to her sister: "Lennox just called me. She told me she has divorced Fredrick and closed up her store and left Toronto. She said it was all very sudden. She is now living in Switzerland. She said she moved there to protect her finances from procurement through investigations. Do you think the United States government is still looking for her after so much time has passed?"

Sara Lee liked drama and was drawn to people who were unsavory. She enjoyed being the liaison for the two families and the feeling of power it gave her.

"Why did Lennox have to leave Canada, Sara Lee? I thought she enjoyed her beauty shop and spa," Mother asked.

"She had to leave because she had not paid her bills in four months. I called her sister and she told me the spa closed overnight. When her employees and customers came that morning for their appointments the store was deserted. She and Jordan are gone."

Six months later:

"Yes, Ruth. Lennox called me last night from Switzerland. She is getting married again! I think this will be husband number four. She told me she met an expatriate from her village in England. He saw her at the bank and approached her. She told me they are moving to Costa Rica and he is going to help her start up her beauty salon there. So, our girl is on the move again."

Lennox was living in a suburb of San Jose, Costa Rica when Interpol finally caught up with her. She had been married only one year when she was arrested. She and her son, Jordan, had opened a spa in Escazu, a community of ex-patriots in a suburb south of San Jose, Costa Rica. She fought the extradition, saying she was not the person they claimed she was, having both a Canadian and a British passport. She explained to the officials, "Look, the numbers on your complaint from the United States Marshal's Office, they are not the same as my passport's name or numbers."

By this time, she had accumulated more than seven last names. When Interpol arrested her, her new husband reported to the paper that he felt she was innocent and he was standing by her side one hundred per cent. Does that sound familiar?

Lennox was being held in a women's prison near San Jose, called El Buen Pastor (translated as The Good Shepherd), considered one of the worst prisons in Costa Rica. With her past record of leaving countries, the court would not grant her bail. Lennox shared a cell module with forty other inmates at El Buen Pastor. She slept in a bunk bed, was only allowed family visitation four hours per week, had no access to the internet, and shared a public phone with her cell mates which only allowed phone calls within Costa Rica. Like other such facilities in the country, the prison had no hot water, meals were basic, and those who were able, usually preferred to have family or friends deliver their food. There was one doctor who was responsible for over eight hundred inmates.

The United Kingdom consular officials visited her there but were not concerned for her welfare. Lennox had convinced her new husband that this was a misunderstanding and they had the wrong person.

Chapter Twenty-Two

THE SENTENCING

There is nothing permanent except change.

— HERACITUS

After ten years, Zach received a call from Interpol telling him Lennox was in Chicago. The agent told Zach his ex-wife was being held at the Metropolitan Correctional Center downtown and was going to be sentenced the following day.

Therefore, in my fifties, I accompanied my parents to the Dirksen Federal Building to see my sister-in-law's sentencing. I felt my blinders came off on this day because I saw my parents for the first time in my life. What I experienced was a strange charade of movements and comments that I never paid attention to before. From the moment we entered the lobby of the Dirksen center to the moment we were seated in the oak paneled courtroom, my parents never stopped talking about poor Lennox.

Sitting in the cold courtroom for hours that day, I had my epiphany. After so many years in my mother's shadow, I finally understood her true nature. I realized how similar my mother and former sister-in-law ultimately were. Mother truly admired Lennox, perhaps even envied her. I suddenly realized they were chameleons. They both were able to change the color of their skin to blend in with their surroundings as they stalked their prey. They watched and waited for hours, years, until they finally could pounce and devour. And I felt that I had been devoured!

On this day, I saw the two women as accomplished actresses who were able to spin their ordinary life stories into larger-than-life fantasies—talking with a pinch of truth and with such flair that it was impossible not to believe them.

To the outside world, the two women appeared to have integrity, they both dressed well and held themselves apart from and above the rest. They were both good interrogators. They'd look you straight on with sincerity, giving the impression they really cared about what you were telling them. However, after they walked away from the person they had just built up, they would degrade them to the next person they met. The two women were generous with gifts, which made people feel beholden to them. For so many years, I watched them operate and wondered if this was normal behavior. It had to be, didn't it? It was all that I knew.

After the clerk announced to the courtroom that Lennox's proceedings were going to be delayed until four, my parents decided perhaps it was time to eat. However, they did not want to relinquish their seats, thinking that a crowd was sure to arrive. My parents usually dined on a schedule with lunch at noon and dinner at five. With nothing else to do, they decided it was time for an afternoon snack.

"Gail, here's a twenty—go downstairs and buy us coffee and some sweets."

"I don't think you can bring food into the courtroom, Dad. I noticed a sign on the outside door." Then I got up with Dad to prove to him there was a notice. Satisfied with the decision to stay, we remained. With nothing else to talk about, we all stared out into space, lost in our thoughts as to what would happen next. Occasionally, they reminisced about their great adventure to England and the moneylender. Then they reflected about Lennox's sense of style, she always dressed so elegantly....

A half hour later, a large man dressed in a dark suit entered the chamber. His size was overwhelming, with the build of a professional football player except for a slight belly. He had wide shoulders, ferocious blue eyes, and long gray hair pulled back into a ponytail. He seemed to be in his sixties. When he walked past us, I could feel a cold breeze.

"I bet that is Lennox's lawyer, David, I am going to go talk to him."

Not missing a beat, Mother got up to approach him. She was never afraid of any man, playing on her charm, beauty, and especially her name. She was Mrs. Dale, of the Dale Uniform Company.

She ran up to Lennox's lawyer, as a groupie does to a star. She looked up at him, introduced herself, and asked if she could speak to the judge on her ex-daughter-in-law's behalf. The lawyer just looked down at her with a snarl and moved past her resembling a football player running out for a pass. Mother, used to getting her way, was infuriated.

"How do you think she is going to look? David, how should we act? Do you think we could talk to her? How do you think I can give her the money?" Mother asked in a rushed whisper that we all could hear.

From the back of the room two twelve-foot oak doors opened, and standing in the threshold was a thin woman dressed in orange clothes. My parents gasped and held on to each other for support. They could not believe what they were seeing. I was mesmerized too. Lennox appeared so small.

She was flanked by two stocky male guards dressed in navy jackets, light blue shirts, navy ties, and worn blue uniform pants. Lennox kept her eyes down as though she were in a trance as she was escorted toward the bench where she was to be seated.

Lennox, as we had known her, was a woman who only wore designer clothes, had a tan complexion, impeccable makeup, and beautiful red long flowing hair. She would never have been seen with men who were not well dressed. We watched her with fascination as she proceeded toward us. She looked so diminutive from where we were sitting just five feet away.

She was dressed in standard-issue prison clothes—a common criminal. She wore a gray sweatshirt under her orange prison top and orange pants. She had on dirty gray sneakers without laces. Her hair was pulled back with a scrunchie. Her hair color was gray at the temples with different washed out colors from there. She wore cheap black plastic glasses and had a drawn, shrunken expression on her face.

"David, I can't believe what I am seeing," Mother whispered as she squeezed her husband's arm. "I was not prepared to see Lennox looking this way."

As she took her seat by her lawyer, she looked down. She did not acknowledge my parents as they had hoped, never glancing our way.

"She saw us, David. How could she not see us? We are the only people in this courtroom."

Mother was speaking loudly, almost shouting, trying to get Lennox's attention. But Lennox choose not to acknowledge them. She sat hunched over in conference with her lawyer.

Mother's heart went out to her ex-daughter-in-law.

"Oh, how Lennox has suffered. She looks so thin. I feel so badly for her. I can't believe this *mishegas* has happened," Mother said, still clenching my father's arm almost in tears.

Her emotions kept fluctuating from excited to mad to sad. All she wanted was to remember the Lennox from the wonderful trip she had organized for them.

"Yes, you can see she has suffered," said Dad. "I cannot believe how she looks, she used to be so regal."

At four o'clock the clerk stood up to announce the judge. We all stood in respect as he was introduced and then proclaimed: "Be seated." The judge took his place at his high bench. I could feel my parents' hearts pumping for soon they would see the Lady.

Lennox and her lawyer stood to face the judge. With their backs to us, it was difficult to hear what was being said.

"I understand you have already pleaded guilty," the judge began, as he shuffled the papers in front of him. "You are charged on four counts: money laundering, wire fraud, conspiracy, and engaging in prohibited financial transactions. During the years of 1985 through 1989, together with six other co-conspirators and companies you created, you devised a scheme to defraud and obtain money and property by fraudulent means from your former employer."

We learned she caused a loss to the brokerage firm of two million four hundred forty-six thousand four hundred ninety dollars. My parents were speechless. Zach had led them to believe the amount was in the thousands, not millions. How could she have obtained so much?

The judge asked if Lennox wished to speak. She was handed a microphone, yet her voice was muffled. We watched as her body quivered as she was talking to the judge, yet we could not hear her much-anticipated response. Her lawyer put his arm around her to keep her steady.

The court proceedings and sentencing only took fifteen minutes. The judge sentenced her to six years in a medium security federal prison. The sentence was reduced by one year, because of the time she had been held in Costa Rica awaiting extradition. She would have to pay a fine of $250,000, or twice the gross loss to the victim, which the government had estimated to be approximately $2,500,00.00, and any other restitution ordered by the court. Her lawyer requested transferring her to a prison in California near one of her sons. This was granted.

As she stepped away from the podium, she became composed. As she moved towards the bench where she had sat before with her lawyer she turned around and smiled in our direction. She blew kisses at my parents and they blew kisses back to her. Lennox was then escorted out of the courtroom by the two guards. We sat still in our seats until we could see her no longer. Then I picked up my parents' coats and we walked out of the courtroom down the hall to wait for the elevator. While we were waiting, her lawyer saw us and my father waved him over.

He shook my father's hand and bowed to my mother, ignoring me.

"Here is my card, my name is Bart Salish. She was really lucky today. She pleaded guilty on all counts and because she spent time in that hellhole in Costa Rica, the judge was lenient. She is going to be sent to a federal facility in California to complete her time. Here is a copy of her plea agreement. Perhaps this will explain to you what happened."

"Thank you," Dad said, "I am the owner of the Dale Uniforms and we also sell men's suits. Please come to my store and let me give you a suit."

"Do you think we will be able to see Lennox? I would like to talk to her and learn about her life since we last saw her?" Mother asked the lawyer.

"I don't know, since the jail is pretty full. I think she is going to be transferred this week. Realistically there probably won't be time."

He said his goodbyes, handed my father the court documents and walked away toward a colleague. We watched him rush off as we waited for the elevator. I couldn't help but feel this day was surreal. It was all happening as if in a dream sequence. My parents locked arms as was their custom and walked down the hall, talking about the lawyer and their plans to meet Zach for dinner. Now that they had the plea agreement, they needed Zach to explain what Lennox's crimes were. But Zach begged off, telling them he was too busy. Russ was asked if he could try to interpret the agreement for them. That night I drove them to our house for dinner.

"OK, I have read it a few times," Russ said with his eyebrows furrowed. He did not want to make any mistakes and be called a dummy by his in-laws. "It says here that Lennox and four other employees of various companies worked with her to create a method to defraud her employer. They created false invoices made out to businesses that did not exist. These are what they call shell companies, existing only on paper. She even created a few herself in Illinois. Then she created invoices, approved the services, and arranged for checks to be drawn and accounted for on the books of her employer in such a way as to deceive the officers and employees of the brokerage firm into believing that the checks were paying for legitimate items or services."

"The second part of the scam happened when Lennox received the checks from the fraudulent companies and gave the check to one of her co-conspirators. The checks were made payable to a company owned and controlled by one of the co-conspirators or herself. Some of the fraudulent company's names were Oxford Tickets, Castle Consulting, and Royal Printing. She does have a theme going, won't you say?" Russ interjected, "In each case, the firm's check was wired to a bank account in England. This is where the wire transfer fraud charge comes in. The co-conspirators then drew a check on the accounts and negotiated it for cash, most often at currency exchanges. Lennox would collect half of all proceeds."

"This explains how she got the money, but is her title real?" Mother asked.

"Do you remember the article I showed you from the *Wall Street Journal*? The article was advertising Lord of the Manor titles. The British government had removed all financial subsidies from families with titles. However, these noble families came up with ways to use their estates to create a series of titles based on land ownership. The nobles would create a deed for a small piece of property, in Lennox's case it measured one meter by one meter. Her title, Lady Bristol, was attached to this piece of land. The nobles also had structures on their land which they would sell as condominiums or convert into hotels. These hotels came complete with butlers, maids, cooks, and support staff to make it seem as though you were living in a royal castle. She had a solid scam going," said Russ as he closed the document and handed it back to my father.

When I asked my parents if they could ever forget the hardship Lennox caused, Mother snapped. "You are heartless girl, Gail. Couldn't you see Lennox's pain today? Wasn't she gracious when she threw us kisses? How sad for the Lady. I felt today she was dethroned," Mother giggled at this last statement as she gave Dad a sideways glance to make sure he was listening to her.

Mother never was able to see Lennox nor give her that ironed one-hundred-dollar bill, but Lennox must have been pleased to see my parents sitting in the courtroom, because the next day they received a handwritten letter from her:

Dear Ruth and David,

I felt I must write this note to you both after this afternoon at the courthouse. First of all, excuse me for not acknowledging you when I first entered, but I knew my emotions would be strong and I did not want to upset myself before my hearing. Our parting all those years ago was not a pleasant one for any of us, but that was the way it went.

In my heart, I want you to know I did love you both, and you were always so loving to my boys. Mixed in with the bad times, I know we did have some very loving family times together. If I did not do all the things you thought I could have done, Ruth, I am truly sorry to you for that. I did my best, and perhaps my way was not correct, but I tried. I think we all got off on the wrong foot with issues very important to you and me, dear Ruth, that never got resolved. The past is the past and I know that now. I look back on these years with many fond memories, never thinking of unhappiness, it would be too painful.

Before I tell you about the boys, I want to say, you both looked WONDERFUL. And I am so happy and yes, I would be proud if I could still look upon you today as my "in-laws." Ruth, to me you look like the same elegant lady. I would not have known ten years have passed since I last saw you. You have been blessed. David, what can I say, the years have been wonderful to you too and I see you are the same. I am so happy for you both that you still have each other.

These last few months here at the detention center, I have not been able to color my hair, but, other than that I am feeling very well. Once more, I compliment you, Ruth and David, on how well you both have kept yourselves.

My sons are my pride and joy and the real loves of my life. As I am sure you know, I have married again, and this is my second divorce since I divorced Zach. My real pleasure has been watching my children grow into young men.

My eldest is 32 years old. He has a thriving business and has become a motivational speaker. He is so handsome and is in love every few months with a different girl. My middle son is 30 years old. He works in construction in British Columbia. He has two children. My youngest child, Dreamy Eyes, as you used to call him, is 28 and lives in Los Angeles. He is in the movie business. He is 6 feet 3 inches tall and so, so adorable. God has given me three wonderful boys and two darling grandchildren, a loving daughter-in-law, and a wonderful husband. So, this is my family and I love them all dearly. We are all very close.

I hope my letter does not bother you in any way. It is not meant to. I just felt I needed to say some things to you.

My sentence today was a kind one, considering it could have been almost four more years. This arrest warrant that happened out of the blue last year came as a surprise to us, but at least I had these past years to help my children grow into fine young men.

With wishes of continued health and happiness to you all, and my sincere best to Zach.

Fondly,
Lennox

EPILOGUE

But when he's dumb and no more here Nineteen hundred years or near, Clau-Clau-Claudius shall speak clear.

— I, CLAUDIUS, ROBERT GRAVES

In the years that followed, we each tried to move on, with varying degrees of success. Not long after things seemed to settle down, Dad's uniform store was embezzled. It was the result of his two favorite employees trying to edge my husband and myself out of the business. Thankfully, with the help of the FBI and the Chicago Police Department, we caught the embezzler, but not before he had caused significant damage. After this, Dad sold his beloved business.

Zach, with the help of our parents, tried to begin again, this time by going to law school. While living in an area of Chicago called Lincoln Park, he was fixed up by our cousin and married an actress named Sloan. He paid to have her teeth capped and bought her a tanning bed. He went shopping for clothes with her and convinced her to dye her hair red. Apparently, change comes hard for some people.

Mother seemed to miss and think about Lennox every day. She spent much of her time writing books about all the experiences she had with her, but she could not finish them. With the help of her son and new daughter-in-law, she hired a ghostwriter to finish the tale, so that she could tell the world about her adventures with Lady Bristol. But even the ghostwriter could not complete her stories, because the reality seemed too preposterous to explain.

That "reality"—the one that kept us preoccupied for so long—may have been preferable to what happened later. Seeing each of my parents decline in ways that are still too painful to talk about, made me wonder if the illusions of the past were what made their earlier life worth living.

As for me, I ended up fending off lawsuits from my dear brother after our parents passed away. Let's just say things didn't end well for him.

Lawyers, friends, cousins—they all said that with time, the battles and recriminations would fade. Not exactly, I must say. Some things are just too deep. One day, just as we were settling into our hard-earned retirement, I received a call from Costa Rica. It was Lennox...

APPENDIX

MY MOTHER'S JOURNAL: THE ADVENTURES OF A LIFETIME.

At last we arrived at London's Heathrow Airport, a bit late, three hours to be exact. Jetlag had set in and we were all tired. Bleary-eyed, we went through British customs. When we saw Lennox and Zach waiting for us, we perked up. Lennox was looking impeccable, gorgeous, slim, and radiant in the light. She stood out in her Scottish clan plaid skirt of green and red. Her long red hair draped down her back, and it was topped, as was her custom, with a matching plaid hat. I noticed right away a huge diamond stickpin fastened to her collar. I looked down at myself. My gray suit looked wrinkled and I suddenly realized my hat was out of style. At least I was wearing my six-carat diamond ring that David bought me for our thirty-fifth wedding anniversary. As our group proceeded out of the airport terminal, I noticed how Lennox commanded a man dressed in a black suit to retrieve our luggage.

"David, did you see that."

"What?"

"Did you notice how Lennox, I mean, the Lady spoke to that man."

"Yes honey, I heard her call him James, I believe he is her chauffeur."

"Her chauffeur. Are we dreaming?"

When we emerged at the car loading area, James was standing in front of a shiny black Mercedes-Benz sedan.

"David, that car, do you think it is for us?" I could not believe my darling son was now living the life he dreamed of and was taking me along. James opened the door to the Mercedes and Lennox came out to tell us to get into the vintage white taxi with the black bumper and bonnet behind them. I looked at my sister and we both slid into the taxi as though it was the most natural thing for us to do, all the while, laughing with joy.

Lennox took David aside, "Please tell Ruth, Sara, and Barney we will be following you to the hotel. The chauffeur has placed your luggage in another taxi."

To be honest, I became disappointed that I was not going in the chauffeur-driven Mercedes with Zach, but the anticipation of riding in a genuine London taxi, being in England, and staying at the famous Connaught Hotel took the edge off.

How I love to educate my family. I told David, Sara Lee, and Barney what I had read about the Connaught. "I learned it is a five-star Edwardian establishment located in Mayfair Village. It is named after Queen Victoria's seventh son, Prince Arthur, the Duke of Connaught. In 1935, the Connaught was run as an English private house, with people of great wealth living there and expecting a high standard of service. And now, thanks to Lady Bristol, we will be given this opportunity to see how high-class Britons are treated and pampered." I was so excited I elbowed Sara Lee in the conspiratorial way that we, as sisters, share.

"Perhaps we will meet Princess Diana, the Queen Mother, or maybe Queen Elizabeth herself." We both laughed.

When the taxi driver turned the corner onto Mount Street, the hotel was the focal point. The Edwardian white porch contrasted with the red brick façade of the six-story building, which wrapped around the corner. David became very excited when he saw the doorman wearing a long morning jacket in taupe with a dark brown fur collar, completed by a matching hat that reminded him of his beloved police hat.

Suddenly, David, I believe, started to think about selling uniforms here. He started speaking to the doorman before he opened the door, "Hello, your uniform fits you so well. Is there a uniform store nearby?"

But the doorman's only words were, "Welcome to the Connaught" spoken with a gorgeous English accent. Sara Lee and I were laughing again. It is so like

David to only be thinking about business. As we left the cab, our first surprise was that Lennox had already taken care of the fare.

We were ushered into the lobby by the bellhop. I do believe our mouths fell open when we saw the opulence that was before our eyes especially the heavy front doors leading into the lobby and the large medieval portraits that lined the dark wood staircase. Sara Lee whispered to me, "Sister, we must look so strange to the people in the lobby. Here we are wilting in our traveling clothes surrounded by piles of luggage and there stands Lennox looking so regal. We look like ragamuffins in the middle of all this grandeur." We looked each other over and laughed at our appearance as we stood waiting for our instructions from Lennox.

Sara Lee was intelligent, she had done very well in school and was a voracious reader, unlike me. She enjoyed reading English novels, which was her link to Zach. Her intellectual comments were always entertaining to him, and she loved it when he smiled at her and gave her a little hug. Sara Lee had been married four times and she had no children of her own, so Zach was the son she wished was hers.

Lennox waved us over to her. I could tell she was going to give us the rules.

"Mom, Dad, Sara Lee, Barney, I want you to know I am going all out on this trip."

As we stood in front of her like adoring puppies, exhausted from the thirteen-hour trip, we wanted her to be as proud of us as we were of her. We listened to her next words in a dreamy haze.

"The experience we are going to have for the next three weeks is all on me, my treat. I don't want you to be uncomfortable, so I am telling you now I am paying for all the accommodations, meals, and transportation. I want you all to have a wonderful experience."

She said this with her hands crossing her chest. I could see my David's eyebrows go up. He never expected this, he was always the one paying. He was surprised, relieved, and then really glad he didn't have to convert American dollars into British pounds.

"You are going to experience a noble person's life as it happens in Britain. I know everything will be foreign to you and you may find it strange. Because of our differences in culture, I want to give you some rules, Please do not point at or talk to anyone here. No one here wants to know about your life in America or hear your business stories."

She said this looking straight into David's eyes. When I saw this, I know my eyebrows went up.

"People are private and do not want to be questioned."

I believe this comment was meant for me. And I felt my eyes lower.

"If they should want to share information with you, they will, but remember, you are with me. Therefore, you represent me and this is my country, so please do not embarrass me."

With this said, she smiled her royal smile and dismissed us with a fluttery movement of her hand. Turning again to the reservation desk, she had some last-minute instructions to leave for the hotel staff. I believe she was making sure our suites and lunch plans were in order.

Lennox had secured the Connaught Suite for David and me, and a regular room for Sara Lee and Barney. Zach and his Lady were staying in the Prince Suite, a huge room with a sitting area overlooking the hotel's charming garden. While we were waiting for Lennox, who was lining up the bellmen to escort us to our suites, I noticed an older woman sitting alone reading the paper. Suddenly my long plane trip caught up with me, I felt tired and decided to sit down next to this woman, who looked a little lonely. Always chatty by nature I introduced myself.

"Hello, my name is Ruth. We just arrived here from Chicago."

The woman paused just long enough to freeze me with a look. She then abruptly went back to reading.

Lennox saw what was happening from the corner of her eye and quickly walked up to us. She bowed her head to the older woman and took me firmly by the arm as she excused herself.

"What were you doing?" she demanded, "I just told you not to talk to anyone. That woman you were annoying is a Duchess and she does not speak to common people like you. We are going to be going to very famous places. There will be royalty and celebrities staying where we have reservations. I do not want to see nor hear you bother them. There will be no talk of flea markets, or uniforms, or Barney going on about cars. Also, please remind David and Barney not to talk to James, my chauffeur. James is on loan to me from my father, the Duke. So, don't try to be chummy with him. Word gets around."

"Most importantly, while we are here, you must address me respectfully as Lady Bristol."

"Of course, Lady Bristol." I instinctively gave a slight bow. These rules were all so new to me and I had never been reprimanded before. The Lady eyed all four of us and sashayed away. I wanted to cry.

"David, Sara Lee, Barney, did you hear what she said? Am I that bad?"

"No, that is crazy. What kind of a rule is that?" Sara Lee answered with a shrug of her shoulders. She has always been there for me—the Ethel to my Lucy.

"I think Lennox is right," David said in a thoughtful manner. "We are on her turf now, so we need to play by her rules. Remember, if you don't do this, this will become a long three-week trip."

I looked at David in disbelief. Was he siding with Lady Bristol? David was my biggest advocate, so maybe he knew something Sara Lee and I didn't. "OK" I said, "I will try to play by her rules. But you know me, it is going to be really hard."

David and I were given instructions to freshen up and meet in the lobby in one hour. The bellhop escorted us across the dark wood-paneled lobby to the lift, and then down a blood-red carpeted hallway to the Connaught Suite. As we approached the suite, a butler was waiting for us at the door.

"Good afternoon Mr. and Mrs. Dale." He bowed. "I am at your service while you are with us at the Connaught. My name is George. Please call for me when you need anything. Here is a list of my services while you are here. Please look it over."

We were impressed and speechless. As we entered our suite, George gave us a tour and demonstrated all the features of the room. He offered us something to drink and invited us to sit down on the plush emerald couch. We watched in amazement as he opened our suitcases and put away our clothes.

"I feel a bit off-balance at this extravagance. I know we are really tired from the trip, David, but I feel as though we are sharing a dream. How will we ever be able to go back home?"

We washed up and changed into our clothes for lunch. We were going to have lunch in the hotel's famous bistro, the Espelette.

"Ruth, I am not sure what fork to use." So typical of David.

The meal was lovely, but we were all jet-lagged. Sara Lee and Barney went up for a nap.

"Tonight I have a special treat planned," Lennox told David and me. "Zach and I will be coming from a cocktail party. Please be waiting in the lobby at eight sharp and be dressed in your evening attire."

At eight o'clock sharp, we were waiting at the front door of the Connaught, chatting with the doorman, David was wearing the one tuxedo he had brought from the Dale Uniform store. I wore the black Gucci gown I had bought on sale at Bonwit Teller. I was also wearing a string of pearls in the manner of Coco Chanel.

Just then, a silver Rolls Royce pulled up with James driving. Out came Zach, wearing a short dark navy jacket, a white shirt with matching plaid tie and cummerbund, and a blue plaid Scottish kilt with the traditional pouch called a sporran suspended from a silver chain. Finishing off the ensemble, he wore knee socks held up by fancy garters and evening dress brogues.

He looked at us with a shy smile on his face as he turned to hold out his hand for his Lady. As Lennox emerged from the car, David and I were stunned by how beautiful she looked—just like a movie star. On this night, she was wearing a silver evening gown with diamond jewelry. The lights from the street only magnified her beauty, as she appeared to float toward us.

David did not know what to say, so he blurted out, "I didn't recognize the car. What happened to the black Mercedes from this morning?"

The Lady and Zach just smiled and giggled as they ushered us into the limo. Only the chauffeur responded to David's question as he tucked him into the back seat.

"Tonight, the Lady required silver," he said in a hushed tone.

"Mom, Dad, our first stop will be at a little elegant restaurant I know called Le Richelieu. After dinner, we'll be going to see "The Phantom of the Opera."

These were the hardest tickets to get anywhere in 1988. Our daughter-in-law had performed yet another miracle, and life was just getting better and better.

When we arrived at the theater, there was a huge crowd standing constrained behind velvet ropes. This was the premiere, complete with a red carpet, security, and photographers. Crowds of people were clamoring to see celebrities. When the silver Rolls pulled up in front, James opened the door for us. It almost didn't feel safe to get out of the car, but we did, pushed along by the excitement of the moment as we walked down the red carpet.

At the entrance to the theater, we turned around to watch for Zach and the Lady.

When Zach got out in his kilt, the crowd gave a scream. Then the Lady emerged from the car, she smiled but did not "wave." We could hear people in the *crowd asking, "Who are they?" We watched intrigued as they paused briefly for pictures before walking arm in arm into the theater.*

We took our seats in the fourth-row center and then were swept away by the performance. I could see why "Phantom" was such a phenomenon.

The night wasn't over. The Lady had James take us by the Tower Bridge, Soho, and the House of Parliament. As Lennox sat back in her seat, she looked secure in the knowledge the evening she planned was perfect. We were having the most marvelous time. We continued past Buckingham Palace, St. James Palace, Marlborough House (where the Queen Mother resides), Piccadilly Circus, Trafalgar Square, and finally, the Tower of London. The entire time, Lennox narrated the history of each important stop.

"You are a wonderful guide and hostess," I said to Lennox. "I can't thank you enough for the evening."

"Oh, it's not over yet. James, stop at the pub on the corner."

I looked at Lennox and started to wonder who she was. Here, as in Chicago, she was in command, but in London, in this setting, I was seeing another side of her personality. She really was regal! When the car stopped, she said, "This is a four-hundred-year-old pub, it is located near a clock I know you will recognize."

And just then Big Ben chimed midnight. It was the perfect ending to an enchanting night.

In the morning, we were woken up by a soft knock on the door. David got up and put on the luxurious Connaught robe and matching slippers.

"Ruth, this is so strange. We have never stayed in a hotel like this, yet I feel right at home."

As he opened the door there stood George, the butler. He wheeled in a breakfast trolley.

"I didn't order this," David said nervously. He would never spend money to have food delivered to his room.

"Yes, I know Mr. Dale. Lady Bristol did."

The butler lifted the lids on a selection of fresh juice, croissants, porridge, jams, toast, a platter of cut fruit, coffee, and cream, and said, "If there is something else you would like please tell me and I will fetch it for you."

"No, I think we will be more than fine. Thank you" David closed the door as I ran to look at the food.

We own a lakefront condo on a prestigious street in Chicago, two vacation homes, various rental properties, real-estate holdings, and a growing stock port-

folio, but we also grew up in the shadow of the Great Depression. So as much as we enjoyed this luxury, it was also a little disorienting.

"Let's eat" I said to David. "Lennox told us to be ready by eleven. We are going to Kings Cross Railway Station for the seven-hour trip to Aberdeen, Scotland, and we are changing trains to continue to Inverness."

Lady Bristol was waiting for us at the station and stood talking to the chief porter about the itinerary. Zach helped organize us onto the palatial seats of our railway carriage.

The trip to Aberdeen passed quickly. Before we realized it, the noon hour was upon us. Lennox had the Connaught Hotel prepare a picnic lunch laden with scrumptious sandwiches, wine, and rich chocolate desserts.

"Oh, I can see my waistline expanding," Sara Lee said, as she looked out the window admiring the picture-book houses with their small meticulously manicured gardens, as she put away two cucumber sandwiches with the crust cut off.

David and I sat admiring Zach, looking so handsome and happy, kissing and speaking softly to the Lady.

At Aberdeen Station, we proceed to the Isle of Skye. Upon arriving at the transfer station and looking towards the distance, we heard the sound of bagpipes permeating the air. In the distance, we saw a thin woman leading the men towards the train.

"Is that Lennox?" Sara Lee asked.

"Yes, I think so," David responded.

"When did she change clothes?" Barney commented.

"When did she leave the train?" I said as I looked out the window.

Lennox was dressed in a red plaid kilt, a red form fitting suit jacket with a little red plaid cap with yellow and red pom-poms on the top. She was standing in front of the Highland Prince. With a huge smile on her face she beckoned us.

"This Jacobite steam engine with its matching coaches is called the Highland Prince." Lennox spoke with her heaviest accent, screaming above the sound of the bagpipes.

"I have hired this private three-car train just for us. Kings and Queens have sat here and now it is your turn."

She then turned towards our Zach, gave him her hand, and seemed to float up the three steps into this majestic train.

The four of us moved as if in a trance. When we entered the private train, its ancient charm took our breath away. Zach seemed to take this experience as though he had done it many times before.

"The blue and green plaid curtains are so vintage, I feel as though I am on the Orient Express. Do you think Hercule Poirot, the sleuth, is on board?" Sara Lee, ever the reader, asked Zach.

"Look at the seats Ruth, your favorite white lace doilies for our heads." Sara Lee pointed out. The fireside, or wingback chairs, were of the same color as the curtains, blue and green checked. The chairs were not facing the windows but rather they faced inward giving the appearance of being in a person's living room.

"The chairs look so elegant and cozy with their side wings. I think I heard Lennox call them checks." I tried to sound educated as well.

On the little tables that separated the chairs were crisp white tablecloths and the small glass crystal vases held fresh deep purple thistles, the symbol of Scotland. On the dark mahogany walls hung oil paintings of Scottish landscapes. Each painting was illumined with a soft overhead light giving the train car the impression of being lit by candles. Each little bathroom was appointed with the finest toiletries, and the Highland Prince crest was on everything.

The train took us through a panorama of rolling green hills that were dotted with sheep and cows.

"As these little towns rolled by, it makes me think of Wisconsin. "I looked at David for confirmation.

"Yes, isn't it interesting to look out the window and forget we are thousands of miles from home," David said, looking homesick already.

Lennox had hired a chef from the Cordon Bleu to prepare our dinner. Chef Michael came out of the kitchen dressed in starched whites to tell us about the meal he planned for the evening.

When the wine was served, I felt I must give a toast.

"On behalf of all of us, the lucky adventurers, I would like to thank our gorgeous daughter-in-law, the fabulous Lady Bristol and my most handsome son for an unforgettable experience. Personally, I feel like a princess."

Late in the evening, the train arrived in Inverness. A car and driver transported us to the Kings Mill, a five-star hotel.

Lennox once again became our tour guide. "William Inglis was the Provost of Inverness and he built this hotel in 1786."

Sara Lee and I gave each other knowing glances, we were so impressed because Lennox knew this information by heart.

"This hotel is famous for two reasons, Robert Burns, the national poet of Scotland, had slept here in 1787, and it is close to Loch Ness where the famous Loch Ness Monster is said to live. Loch is a Gaelic word meaning lake. It really can mean any major body of freshwater. You will notice how green and lush this area is tomorrow morning."

Lennox smiled at us, her American family, she must have known we were in awe of her.

"We will stay at this inn for two days," She said as she handed out the keys to our rooms.

David and I walked with the bellhop to our suite overlooking the rose garden. Looking out the window, we decided to take a beauty walk together. We walked in silence, holding hands, trying to think of how to express our emotions but not finding the words. When we returned to our room and went to bed, I could hear David crying.

"What's wrong David? Don't you feel well? I know we have been eating a lot."

"No, I am ok. I just miss my bagel and cream cheese breakfast. I am not used to this type of living and it makes me nervous."

I looked at him with love, because only I would be able to understand his reasoning.

At eight-thirty in the morning our group was assembled once again for the next trek of the journey. Lennox appeared in a dark green burnt orange sweater, jeans, and gray Wellington boots. Attached to the side of her luxurious red hair was a checkered cap. The rest of us were dressed in the same clothes we wore the day before. David and Barney were wearing their blue pants with sweaters, Sara Lee always in Burberry, me, in a gray pleated shirt and sweater, and Zach in his green mackintosh and blue jeans.

We took the same seats on the train car as the day before.

"Our next stop is the Isle of Skye," Lennox told us. "The isle population is around eight thousand, it is about fifty-seven miles long, twenty–seven miles wide, and the entire isle is shared with around forty thousand sheep. You will notice the sheep have their own coat of arms on their bums. Ok, that is enough information for today, enjoy the trip."

When we arrived at the station, it was mid-afternoon. There was a deluxe *mini-bus waiting and we were whisked away out to the countryside of the island. We walked through the open meadows only occupied by snobby sheep with their elitist tattoos.*

"David, I feel like we have left the planet. The air smells so sweet here. Take a deep breath. I think the air smells so clean because of the sea and did you notice there are no people in sight?"

When we reached a clearing, the Lady turned and said, "I hope no one minds, I thought we could dine al fresco."

Suddenly, we heard a car and as we looked into the horizon, a green station wagon drove up, two male waiters dressed in black morning coats with white gloves appeared, and were carrying all the necessities for a picnic.

I looked at David with tears rolling down. "This is another moment I will never forget." David hugged me, because he too could find no words for what we were experiencing.

"Take it easy Mother. You are making too much of this trip," said a happy Zach as he was eating his foie gras on a cracker and drinking red wine from a crystal glass. David and I looked at each other in shock. How could Zach not be impressed?

The next day, we boarded the Highland Prince as though we had done it every day of our lives. We resumed our chosen seats and prepared to watch the landscape fly by. When we arrived at Aberdeen station, Lennox had again arranged for three cars—a Renault station wagon to take the luggage, another to take us, and a Land Rover for them.

"Today's destination is Hatton Castle in Turiff near Aberdeenshire. This is where my party is going to take place. We have time so let's take the Edinburgh route," Lady Bristol instructed the driver.

The trip to Hatton Castle would take approximately forty-five minutes and she wanted to show us more of her country. Lady Bristol instructed the driver to give her family a tour of the capital city. As we passed the Queen Mother's estate, the reality of this experience really hit me. I had been daydreaming about meeting the Queen Mother, perhaps my daughter-in-law had another surprise up her sleeve, which would be a great chapter in this journal. The Renault traveled on back roads of the country through narrow streets. Many times, the four of us felt nervous when we passed another car going the opposite direction, but the Lady just laughed when we expressed our fear.

"A miss of an inch is as good as a mile," she told us as she flipped her hand, the one now sporting a five-carat ruby.

I was looking out the window watching the scenery change. I had just fallen asleep when I felt the car take a turn into a long winding driveway. When I opened my eyes, I could not believe the castle that was in front of me. It looked as though it had been painted onto the landscape. It was everything a castle should be. Once again, Cinderella came to mind because the castle was pink in color and had many pointed pitches. On the tip of the towers there were ornaments in gold twirling in the breeze and some of the towers had colorful flags with dominant crests. The building looked like it could have fallen from the sky. David looked at me and in concert we said Brigadoon, our favorite play about an entire town coming to life for only one day every one hundred years.

Now it was Zach's turn to educate us.

"The castles in Scotland were built with military purposes in mind and were the homes of lords or nobles."

Zach paused to make sure we were awake and listening.

"The word castle in Latin, means fortified place. The locations of the castles are found in spectacular locations. They can be perched on the very edges of cliffs with the ocean pounding the rocks, on an island, or near ancient volcanic rock overlooking heather glens. Scottish castles are tied to clans and the Scottish monarchy. Each clan would have a castle where the clan chief and his family would live. Many were built during the period between the 11th and 14th centuries. Hatton Castle's design is Georgian. Georgian style is a simple two-story box. This castle looks pink, but most castles are gray because they reflect the stone from the area."

As we drove up, an enormous steel gate opened, and a row of servants appeared. The staff of the Laird came out and lined up. There was the butler, the housekeeper, the cook and her three assistants, the first-floor maid, and the second-floor maid. They were all dressed appropriately. The ladies in their black dresses with their starched white aprons and caps, and the men in black suits. Lady Bristol walked up to the staff and standing in true glory of her new pedigree, spoke to them in her strong proper British accent. I thought there was a royal glow about her as I watched her with a huge parental smile of satisfaction.

"I want everyone to meet my husband Dr. Dale and his parents, Mr. and

Mrs. Dale. I would also like to introduce you to Dr. Dale's Aunt and Uncle, Mr. and Mrs. Kaplan."

As we walked down the line the household staff each expressed their happiness at being able to serve Lady Bristol's family. Then the butler took over and gave us a tour of Hatton Castle, he began:

"This castle is owned by Laird and Lady Cuff. You will meet them tomorrow. There are fifty-two rooms in all," the butler, Alfred, explained in his very British accent, "each room is equipped with modern conveniences. The first house built on this land in the 1300s was called Balquholly, that house was razed. Ancestors of the present Laird built Hatton Castle in 1745. It had been remodeled extensively in the 1800s. Subsequently, it had electricity installed and modern-day lavatories."

"Do you think all castles have the same decorator?" Sara Lee whispered to me. "They all seem to have old portraits of family members, deep paneled walls, silver everywhere, and endless halls. Do you think this castle has any ghosts?"

"If they do, I hope they are friendly," David quipped in.

As the days went by, we were becoming accustomed to the life of luxury but always nervous we would make a faux pas. When lunch was announced and we were seated in the grand dining hall, we did not know how to behave so we sat with our hands folded on our laps waiting for instruction from the Lady. The dining table was set with museum quality china and the silver flatware was stamped with the Cuff Crest. David was so nervous he poured salt in his water glass. Sara Lee and I wanted to laugh but knew better, so we covered our mouths with the triple size cream linen napkins. Nevertheless, Lennox saw the whole episode and gave us glaring stares.

We learned through Alfred that the Cuff's rent out their eight-bedroom castle and provide entertainment for their guests. The types of entertainment available were shooting, stalking, fishing, tennis, golf, and visits to ancestral homes and distilleries. Because everything we wanted to do was there, we felt comfortable and not rushed. Alfred, and the staff served us just like we had seen on the episodes of "Upstairs Downstairs," a British series on television.

Breakfast was served in the breakfast room, which was full of light and flowers. When the staff served us kippers, a type of herring, it sent us into peals of laughter, for herring was a staple in our household too, but calling it kippers gave it a tastier ring. Finally, Zach joined us for breakfast because Lady Bristol was busy preparing for her forty-first birthday party. The three of us played tennis like old times and went for long walks on the property.

"Oh, Zach, this is all so incredible. I cannot believe how beautiful it is here. Dad and I are so happy for you. You have been with Lennox for eight years now. We have been so worried. It seemed to us that nothing she told us was true. Yet, here we are standing in this green pasture with ducks roaming around and sheep in the distance. I am so grateful this all worked out for you."

That evening, we were told to be dressed in formal attire and be waiting at the entrance of the castle lawn at seven o'clock sharp, for the birthday celebration. When the four of us arrived at the appointed location, there were about twenty people congregated. We introduced ourselves to Lady Bristol's solicitor, Miles; and his secretary, Millie; the Lady's decorator, Finn; and her groundskeeper, Duncan. Her father, Peter, was there standing alone with a cigar and scotch in hand. Peter looked at us and waved but did not come forward to say cheers. The rest of the guests who were invited were the craftsmen who worked for Lennox.

At seven-thirty, Zach appeared dressed once again in a deep green clan kilt with matching hat and socks. Next to him stood Lennox in a vintage evergreen satin form fitting dress with a diamond pin holding the side of her hair back. We heard the now familiar sounds of bagpipes drifting toward us from the east. Twelve bagpipe soldiers in band formation dressed in matching clan dress kilts appeared in the mist, coming towards us on the stone covered driveway. Following them were the Lairds of neighboring castles along with their English Setters barking to keep the beat.

I looked at Zach, and felt his dream life come true. I could feel his heart beating with happiness.

"David, look at the kids. They are clapping to the rhyme of the bagpipes. They look so happy, so lovely. This is another moment I will remember forever."

"I thought she could never top her fortieth birthday, but this is unreal," Sara Lee slid over to where we were standing so that she could share my view of the couple.

The performance continued for half an hour. We applauded with true delight when it was over because we were starting to get headaches.

Lennox and Zach led the way back into the main dining room where the table was laid out for the gala birthday party. When she blew out the candles on her three-layered chocolate cake, she turned to her guests.

"I would like to show everyone the gift my husband, Dr. Dale, gave me for my forty-first birthday," She said as she pushed her sleeve back for all to see a sparkling diamond bracelet.

I looked at David and could see he was confused.

"How could Zach afford to buy a diamond bracelet?" we asked each other at the same time.

"How lucky to have a daughter-in-law who is wealthy, surely Lennox purchased it for herself and is just giving Zach the credit." I said to him as I patted his hand to try to calm him down. I did not want to spoil the mood of the party, I chose the high road.

As I was trying to cover a possible explosion from David, the Laird of the Castle rose from his chair to announce in his baritone voice,

"Ladies and Gentlemen, it is time to adjourn to the Great Hall where we will be entertained by young Highland Fling dancers."

The next morning, it was time to leave. We said our goodbyes to the staff as they lined up outside the entrance. There were two Ford Granada's waiting to take us to another country chateau.

"I hope you enjoyed my party. I think it went rather well." Lennox began, "Today I have instructed the driver to take you to see Balmoral Castle so you can view the summer home of Queen Elizabeth II."

Once again, I began to fantasize about meeting the Queen. David thought about talking to the Queen's guards to ask where they buy their uniforms and emblems. Barney was busy looking at all the old cars, and Sara Lee was always looking for a place to eat.

"Today's itinerary: we are going to spend the night and have dinner at Macdonald Linden Hall in Northumberland. It is about a half hour drive from there to see our Castle Callaly. This is the castle I am having remodeled for us to live in." The Lady told us this as she closed our car door and proceeded to her Lamborghini.

The drive to Macdonald Linden Hall took us through rolling hills with panoramic scenes of the mountainside. White sea gulls were making their nests on all sides of the mountain off the North Sea. We saw old iron and stone gates that looked as though they went on forever.

"When we return home, I am going to try to paint this," I said to our group, "Have you ever seen anything so beautiful?"

The night before, Lady Bristol told us about her castle. "Callaly Castle is located in Whittingham, ten miles west of Alnwick, where we will spend the night. I had to sell Hartington Castle, the one the Duke gave me. It turned out it was too small, and I did not care for the location. Callaly is still being renovated. Therefore, you will not be able to go inside. But we can walk the grounds. They are really spectacular. The style of the castle is called Jacobean, named after King James of England."

"Oh, that was the same style of the train we were on," I blurted out, to show I had been paying attention.

"Yes, you are right Ruth. Good for you. Well, King James, who was a disciple of new scholarship, influenced the change of house design. So, there are motifs of German and Flemish carvers in the mansion. It is now being subdivided into four private apartments. The castle was built in the 17th-19th century, it incorporates a medieval peel tower dating back to the 12th century, which you can see on the west wing."

After two weeks of touring and staying in castles, our group thought we were experts on royal living, but I think Lennox saw our eyes glazing over. We were all tired and trying hard to be interested. Knowing what would perk us up, she changed her lecture into gossip.

"This castle comes with a story. The Lord of Callaly commenced to building of the castle on the hill, but his Lady preferred to live in the vale. He stubbornly continued to build his castle and she could not persuade him to listen to her. Therefore, she resorted to superstition. She had one of her servant's dress as a boar. She told him to climb the hill at nightfall and pull down all that had been built during the day. It was soon whispered through the dale that spiritual powers were opposed to the work. When the Lord had the work watched one night, the prospect of the boar had become so great in the men's minds that when the boar emerged from the wood the men thought they saw a monstrous animal of great power. The boar cried out among the tumbled stones:

"Callaly Castle built on the height,
Up in the day and down in the night
Built down in the Sheppard's Shaw
it shall stand for aye and never fa"

"This is a quote by George Tait, I believe the date was 1862. I learned this in school."

After Lennox finished her tale, we all applauded.

"Lennox, you really know how to tell a story."

When we arrived at Callaly Castle, Sara Lee and Barney were tired from the ride and decided to remain in the car, while the rest of us got out of the car to explore the grounds. Lennox saw her workmen and left us to discuss her plans. Zach went with us to walk the gardens.

We were not impressed. There were stone boulders casually lying about everywhere, the gardens were overgrown, and the cost to refurbish the castle was not in David's scope of counting.

"I think the fence builders of old were true craftsmen, using the materials of the area to the best advantage. But everything looks overgrown and the mansion appears spooky," I confided to David in a hushed voice.

"I think the building has a good roof," David proclaimed. He was feeling better today because we only had one more week of this trip and then we were going home.

Having Zach to myself for a bit I wanted to talk to him about what I had observed.

"Zach, what does Lennox do when she is not with us?"

"What do you mean, not with us? She is with us every day." Zach spoke harshly to me. He did not like to be questioned.

"Well, she is not around now," I whispered back.

"Oh, please Mother. Leave her alone." Zach turned and walked away.

"What did I say?" I asked David, "Where is she all day? Don't you wonder? We have all been traveling together for two weeks now. I think I can count on my fingers how many times we have seen her. What does she do?"

With our inspection of the Castle completed, we were herded back to the inn. The Lady had prepared a dinner party at seven. She had invited some of her new neighbors to dine with us, sort of a meet and greet. Unfortunately, we were so tired, we all could have used a few hours to rest. Sara Lee and I would have enjoyed a salon and a fresh wardrobe. So, we did our best and promptly at seven, Lennox's entourage arrived at the restaurant.

When we saw Lennox, we felt she put everyone to shame. She appeared in a white suit with pink lilies embroidered on the entire right side of the jacket. The flowers in the room were pink lilies and I had a hard time telling where the flowers stopped and her suit jacket began. Her hair was piled high on her head and there were rows of oyster pearls holding her hair in place. Her makeup was flawless as she gave her royal nod for us to approach her.

"Ruth, David, Sara Lee, Barney, I want you to meet our new neighbors."

Then she went on to introduce them not only by name but by profession. We meet a heart surgeon, a magistrate, a solicitor, a sea captain, banker, and their lovely wives who all had the peaches and cream complexions that Scottish women were known for.

We were escorted into a glass enclosed garden terrace with orchids, lilies, and roses everywhere. The table was arranged on pedestals in the fashion of King Arthur's Knight of the Round Table. In the center of the terrace was an arrangement of spring flowers which had a fragrance that filled the air.

"Please look for your place card Ruth, I sat you next to the sea captain. I thought you would find him interesting."

When I located my seat, I saw there was a lovely pink corsage next to my name. I was so grateful for the corsage because it would cover up the stain I had on my dress. As I looked at the place setting, I saw a hand-written menu.

"Sara Lee, do you think she wrote these menus out herself? When does she find the time? Do you think that is why Zach got mad at me when I asked him what Lennox is doing? I should know better."

"She is amazing. Listen, Ruth, the pianist is playing your favorite, Chopin."

After a parting breakfast in another wing of Linden Hall, we were accompanied by Zach, as Lennox was busy elsewhere, but I was no longer going to second-guess her. Lennox scheduled a tour of Alnwick Castle for us today.

As we entered Alnwick Castle, we all felt a little critical. After visiting and staying at many castles, we all now felt that we were in a position to judge.

"Too big, too much to see," was Barney's comment.

"How did they get it all together, after all the 11th century wasn't that long ago," that was David's.

"No wonder the castle got so big, what good shoppers they were—when they ran out of closet space, they just built on to the castle," that comment was mine.

Sara Lee loved each castle and she especially enjoyed the gift shops.

On August 5th, the trip ended. We found ourselves once again at Heathrow Airport. Our luggage had grown from two bags each to four with a carry on. Our waistlines had also increased. The men purchased suspenders at Heathrow to keep their pants up and Sara Lee and I just did not button the top button on our skirts. Zach was returning to Chicago with us, but Lady Bristol was staying on to work on her castle.

The flight home took almost nine hours. With so much luggage, twenty-six pieces in all, we were worried about getting through customs.

"David, I hope you can get us through. Do you sell uniforms to the customs guards?" Barney asked.

When we approached the customs officer, he looked up from reading Zach's passport.

"Dr. Dale, do you remember me? My wife and I saw you last month in your office. Did you enjoy your stay in England?" and with a warm smile, he let us all go through.

Thus, ends the story that Mother wrote.

ACKNOWLEDGMENTS

This story has taken Russ and me over fourteen years to complete. My mother wrote two books about her experiences with the Lady and my brother. But she always found it too difficult to finish. After all who wants to tell the world how they were "DUPED."

As a child I watched my parents' behavior and would comment on it often to the parents of my friends who lived on our block. But no parent ever said anything, therefore I felt it was normal. I now realize that this retelling of my experiences has really honed in the memories of my life. And this story is as true to me now as it was when I was living it.

Like my mother, I have found this story difficult to complete. I did not want to sound like a "poor little rich girl" and if I come across this way I am sorry. I really wanted to show the literary world how a family can be misguided by how they perceive the American Dream.

Russ and I would like to thank all our friends and professionals who helped us through the years to complete this story: First of all, my mother, who journaled her three-week trip through England and Scotland with the royal couple. And then her final reflections that she typed in all capital letters telling what happened to her son after Lennox left him.

While I was going to DePaul University, I learned about The Writing Center. I went there three times a week for one hour to work on this manuscript. I would like to thank the young woman there who had so much patience with me. However, I apologize as I did not write her name down. This seems to be a theme. I did ask many people to help me craft my words in the most coherent way. I guess I did not believe I would every complete the work.

When Russ retired, we moved to Puerto Rico. One year after we moved here, he fell on the paving stones in Old San Juan and broke his knee cap. Since he could not walk for eight weeks, we decided to spend our time working on the story.

Once he was able to drive, we started to take Spanish lessons. Our teacher, Marlene Aponte, was also an editor. She enjoyed hearing our story and helped us put it in order.

We then hired Jessika Bella Mura. Jessika, also an editor, really helped us fine tune the story. Annika Pfluger was our proofreader and formatted the ebook.

I want to thank my girlfriends who listened while I told them the story and then became my Beta readers. Marla Friedman, Cory Crock, Sheri Ollendorf, Marge Rieff, Susan Lieber, Marisa Ramirez de Arellano, Maureen Headington, Karen Zibell, Carol Sisman, and Renee Smith.

I leave this story for our children Tracy Zirko, Nick Patterson, and their families who lived through this experience with us. I feel this story will be a way for them and their children to know from whence they came.

Hallee Kale Patterson was born in Chicago and Russell Patterson in Tulsa, Oklahoma. Living in Chicago for thirty-five years, they retired and now reside in San Juan, Puerto Rico. Hallee is now writing for "The Weekly Journal" an English language newspaper in Puerto Rico.

Printed in Great Britain
by Amazon